Her breath (reaction to someth....g .... g...s said to him. Certainly his size alone would draw attention. Close-cropped reddish hair, her favorite shade of blue eyes, like his kids', and muscles in that thin T-shirt that teased a woman to knead them with her hands. She had had a hard time concentrating on stage during the first set. Her eyes had sought his involuntarily again and again. And damn if he wasn't sending her appreciative vibes. Must be this crazy heat in April. She extended her lower jaw and blew air up over her face.

Frankenstein called for his bride. Charlotte counted to ten and then ran out from behind the curtain. The crowd jumped to their feet and cheered. Wow, this is what it must feel like to be a rock star. Emi, I think I'm jealous of you. Maybe I should switch careers and we can do a sister act.

Her ego stroked, she enjoyed every minute of the performance. Mummy led the cast off stage into the audience.

"Pick us. Please pick us!" The hunk's kids yelled.

Well, of course I will. Her hips gyrating, she sashayed in his direction, her eyes locked on his heavenly blues.

"Here she comes. She's going to pick us this time."

She averted his eyes and focused on his cute kids. "Hi, girls. Would you like to come up on stage with me?"

"Is it okay, Uncle Pat? Can we please?"

"Sure it is. Go ahead."

Saints be praised. No wedding band on the man's hand, either. "Would Uncle Pat like to come up on stage, too?"

All's Fair
in
Love and Law

The Sullivan Boys, Book Four

by

K. M. Daughters

All's Fair in Love and Law: The Sullivan Boys, Book Four

COPYRIGHT © 2010 by K. M. Daughters

Cover Art by *Kim Mendoza*

The Wild Rose Press
PO Box 706
Adams Basin, NY 14410-0706
Visit us at www.thewildrosepress.com

Publishing History
First Crimson Rose Edition, 2010
ISBN: 1-60154-877-X

Dedication

For Our Parents,
Kay and Mickey, Jeanne and Tom, Violet and Nick

Acknowledgements

Our gratitude to and esteem for our editor,
Joelle Walker, can never be fully expressed.
Joelle informs and inspires our work,
unfailingly raises our spirits
and honors us with her friendship and love.
Joelle, we know your heart, too. And it is beautiful.

Thank you to our Brian, J.D.,
for your insights and lawyering expertise.
Charlie Demarco owes you.

Kudos for K. M. Daughters

AGAINST DOCTORS ORDERS
The Sullivan Boys, Book One
2009 THE Lories, 3rd Place, Romantic Suspense
"Daughters has crafted an intriguing story, full of detailed scenes and fascinating, believable characters. Crisp dialogue and an even balance of action and drama keep the pages turning." (5 Stars)
~WR Potter, Reader's Choice Literary Reviews
"Watch out...the Sullivan Boys are a force to be reckoned with! [This book] packs a punch."
~NY Times Bestselling Author, Brenda Novak

BEYOND THE CODE OF CONDUCT
The Sullivan Boys, Book Two
"Compelling."
~Donna M. Brown, RT Book Reviews
"Ms. Daughters has done it again with a classic romantic suspense read! This story is hot hot hot!"
~Val Pearson, You Gotta Read Book Reviews
"An engrossing and hard to put down story!"
~A. Pohren, Café of Dreams Book Reviews
"Romantic suspense just doesn't get any better!"
~Cheryl Malandrinos, The Book Connection Book Reviews

CAPTURING KARMA
The Sullivan Boys, Book Three
"Compelling, Page Turner..."
~RT Book Reviews
"The author writes with such a warm, flowing style, it's like visiting old friends. You'll want to see what happens next, and hope for only the best."
~Cindy Himler, RT Book Reviews
"Cleverly entertaining...thrilling."
~Geri Ahearn's Book Reviews

Prologue

With a glance at his manicured hands, he caressed the smooth steering wheel. Now this is a birthday present, Father. The Lotus purred and vibrations shimmied up his taut legs as he braked the car at a red light. Not some thousand dollar a night whore. His eyes, like lasers, scanned the deserted sidewalks, searching.

Did you really think that whore could make a man out of me? Why the hell couldn't you just leave me alone? Accept the freak you created. You made the beast, Father. Deal with it.

"That's all? All you got is that tiny, itty-bitty package? It's going to take a lot more than a thousand bucks to make that little gherkin stand at attention." She had laughed until she was gasping for air.

Screw you, bitch. You weren't laughing as I choked the life out of you.

He stroked the grip of the baseball bat propped against the passenger seat. The woman leaning against the building caught his eye. Pulling the car up to the curb, he plucked his driving gloves off the passenger seat.

Batter up.

Chapter 1

Death brought a family closer together. The Sullivan family had twice their share of death lately. *How will we ever get past this? In my book we were close enough already.*

Patrick Sullivan angled an arm and wiped sweat off his forehead with the sleeve of his T-shirt. "Damn, it's hot today."

"Damn is a bad word, Uncle Pat. You are not allowed to say damn. I am telling Mommy that you said damn," Peggy Lynch admonished her uncle with a stern schoolmarm's glare.

"*You* just said damn three times, Peg," Amanda chirped in her twin's ear.

The girls huddled together and giggled.

Their uninhibited laughter, in short supply these days, touched Patrick's heart. Glad he had volunteered for uncle duty, this day at the amusement park might supply the escape Mike's kids needed. The senseless death of their daddy, his brother-in-law, had knocked the slats from beneath the entire Sullivan family.

The girls had encased themselves in a protective shell and had protested leaving their house for any reason. Maybe because when they had returned home a month ago from a carefree hour on the playground, they had walked into the advent of the news of Mike's fatal car crash, the Sullivans in turmoil and their mother temporarily unable to mask her raw grief.

This promised trip to the amusement park was Patrick's less than subtle bribe in cahoots with his brothers. If the twins attended school for an entire week at a time, each uncle in turn would take them anywhere they wanted on Saturdays. Thankful that Danny had suffered through the lunch at the American Girl store and Joe had pulled face painting at the mall, Patrick was relieved to draw the day at the park. Who knew what the girls would come up with for Brian?

"Uncle Pat, can we go on the whirligig again?" The request sounded like one sweetly pitched voice in stereo.

How do they manage to ask the same question at the same time like that?

"You bet we can. Last one in line has to buy the hot dogs." Patrick gave the girls a head start and laughing, jogged in exaggerated slow motion behind them.

After somehow holding down a total of four hot dogs, two cotton candies and one bucket of popcorn in those tiny stomachs, they squeezed in two flights on the whirligig and a spin on the circler between non-stop eating. Chugging a bottle of pop each, the twins finally showed signs of slowing down, scuffing along in their flip-flops.

"Okay, princesses, time to catch your carriage home." He probably had a few more rides left in him, but he wanted to check on Kay.

His sister had remained strong for her children during the funeral of her beloved husband, undoubtedly anesthetized with shock. The pain of loss eventually pierced through the numbness, and the helpless family watched as Kay slipped into depression. Her two elder kids, Mike Jr. and Mary, kept a vigilant eye on their mother. But they needed to be teenagers, not caregivers.

"Can we see the show first?" Amanda's plea came with the cutest, widened sky-blue eyes and cocked head.

"Mommy and Daddy always let us see the Graveyard Rock N Roll Revue before we go home," Peggy insisted with a toss of her blonde ponytail.

These two will be man-killers when they grow up. "The Graveyard Revue? That sounds too scary to me."

"It's not scary, Uncle Pat. Honest." Peggy crisscrossed a tiny index finger over her heart.

Patrick halted on the sun-baked concrete walkway and yanked the crumbled park pamphlet from the back pocket of his snug jeans. Scanning the events listings, he muttered, "Let's see…

"The last show for the day is in a half hour. We have time to get to the other side of the park and find the theater. Are you sure it's not too scary?"

"It's not scary at all, Uncle Pat. We promise." Amanda grabbed his hand and squeezed it.

"Okay, let's go. Does anyone want a pop and a pretzel?" *Couldn't possibly have room.*

"I do."

"I do."

Shows what I know about six-year-olds.

Both girls skipped at his side, holding each of his hands, semi-skimming the pavement as he towed them along with his long strides. The air smelled of roasted meat, fried dough, coconut-scented suntan lotion, and in close proximity, the slightly medicinal sunscreen he had slathered on his nieces' fair faces and arms in the car.

Balancing three large cups and a bag filled with warm pretzels on a cardboard tray, Patrick followed the bouncing girls down gray concrete slab stairs into the bottom of the amphitheatre's bowl.

"Do we have to sit in the front row?" Patrick called.

"Yes!" Amanda hollered back over her shoulder.

Music blared from huge speakers on the stage. The audience clapped in cadence with a pulsating rock beat. Patrick settled the girls on the aluminum bench in the front row and then sat behind them like a shield. Boot heels propped against the rim of the bench on either side of them, he tapped his feet to the infectious beat of the music. He chugged the pop; its fizz stung his parched throat. Egged on by his nieces, Patrick clapped and stomped his feet, too. *Stomp, stomp, clap*...rock you.

The music halted abruptly. Silence.

"Here she comes, Uncle Pat. Here she comes." One of the twins whispered, excited.

"Here who comes?"

A haunting, melancholy female voice filled the theater, streamed straight under Patrick's skin, raising goose bumps on his arms. A shadow moved across the stage behind a gauzy curtain. An explosion sounded and the curtain rose. Two sparkler pyres erupted on each side of a huge gravestone. A hollow, groan-scrape sound effect as the stone slid sideways. *Here she comes, indeed.*

She stole Patrick's breath.

Floor-length black lace hugged her lush body. Blue-black hair curled down her back and swayed seductively as she sauntered across the stage, her smoky voice the perfect instrument for the love ballad. Her eyes roved around the audience and lit on him, the lyrics she sang seemingly an intimate message directed to Patrick. She finished the opening number with a demure curtsey and Patrick surged to his feet, clapping and stomping—Peggy and Amanda apparently on the same page, hopping like human pogo sticks. Thank God, the whistles and ovation of the crowd from behind him proved they weren't alone.

Patrick surveyed the audience over a shoulder as the applause died down and detected males of varying ages focused with rapt attention on the vixen in lace. Relieved he wasn't the only member of his gender reduced to putty so easily, he turned forward.

The stage filled with a succession of "dark" characters introduced by different medley segments. The lady in lace danced the waltz with Dracula, the hustle with Wolfman, the twist with the Mummy and the crowd jumped to their feet again when she and Frankenstein did the macarena and asked everyone to join in.

The girls coaxed Patrick up and he complied good-naturedly even though his hip wiggling six-six frame had to look ridiculous doing the yesterday version of the latter-day hokey pokey. He danced with his nieces while his eyes remained riveted on the stunning woman not more than ten feet away.

The glimpses of tanned skin the lace dress afforded tantalized Patrick. Her violet eyes filled with mischief, he would swear she smiled directly at him. Crushed unreasonably when she left the stage, he sat again. Equally unreasonably, Patrick debated the logistics of finessing her telephone number ten minutes after catching sight of the woman.

"Isn't she beautiful, Uncle Pat?" Peggy's face lit with rapt adoration.

Dazed, he hedged, "Who sweetie?"

"The Bride of Frankenstein, silly," Amanda responded.

"She looks scary to me." He faked a chill and shivered, prompting the girls' giggles.

"Wait 'til we tell Uncle Brian that you're afraid of the Graveyard Revue. Uncle Brian thought the Bride of Frankenstein was beautiful, not scary."

"Well, Uncle Brian better not say anything about me being scared or I might have to tell your future Aunt Matty that he has a crush on the Bride of Frankenstein."

****

Charlotte tugged the black velvet mini-skirt up

over fishnet stockings and then stepped into the frothy red crinoline half-slip spread on the floor, drawing it up underneath the skirt. Gathering her thick hair in a tail with her hand, she lifted it up off her neck and tried to catch a breeze backstage after the costume change. Stopping to check herself in the full-length mirror, she fiddled with the buttons on the black leather bustier. No way to stretch the top buttonhole over that button, so she left it open.

Emily's measurements did not match up with hers. Although identical twins, once they were adults a few differences made it possible to tell them apart. The most glaring that moment was Emily's size B cup compared to her size C. Charlotte's breasts were barely contained in the leather corset. A wry smile twisted her lips. *Better be careful dancing the finale. The last thing Emily needs is to lose this job. And the last thing I need is to be responsible for bringing her trouble again.*

Charlotte didn't mind helping her sister out, considering it the least she could do. Peeking through the curtain, she spied on the hunk in the second row. He leaned over and kissed the crowns of his daughters' heads from behind them. Charlotte smiled, a huge, soft spot in her heart for twin girls and loving fathers. She sighed. *Why are all the good men taken?*

Her breath caught as his smile dazzled in reaction to something one of the girls said to him. Certainly his size alone would draw attention. Close-cropped reddish hair, her favorite shade of blue eyes, like his kids', and muscles in that thin T-shirt that teased a woman to knead them with her hands. She had had a hard time concentrating on stage during the first set. Her eyes had sought his involuntarily again and again. And damn if he wasn't sending her appreciative vibes. *Must be this crazy heat in April.* She extended her lower jaw and blew air up over her face.

Frankenstein called for his bride. Charlotte counted to ten and then ran out from behind the curtain. The crowd jumped to their feet and cheered. *Wow, this is what it must feel like to be a rock star. Emi, I think I'm jealous of you. Maybe I should switch careers and we can do a sister act.*

Her ego stroked, she enjoyed every minute of the performance. Mummy led the cast off stage into the audience.

"Pick us. Please pick us!" The hunk's kids yelled.

Well, of course I will. Her hips gyrating, she sashayed in his direction, her eyes locked on his heavenly blues.

"Here she comes. She's going to pick us this time."

She averted his eyes and focused on his cute kids. "Hi, girls. Would you like to come up on stage with me?"

"Is it okay, Uncle Pat? Can we please?"

"Sure it is. Go ahead."

Saints be praised. No wedding band on the man's hand, either. "Would Uncle Pat like to come up on stage, too?"

"Thanks, but no. I'm good."

"Well I bet you are."

He grinned and boyish dimples creased his fair-skinned cheeks. Her purposely suggestive laugh made him blush. The girls wiggled like puppies following her up the stairs.

Hmmm. Uncle Pat?

****

Peg and Amanda followed the Bride perfectly as if they had practiced the dances. *Wonder how many times they've been to the Graveyard Revue? I can understand their addiction to this thing now.* Patrick appreciated every move his nieces made like a proud stage-dad. He didn't miss a thing about their dancing partner's movements, either—particularly that enticing cleavage.

An unforgettable day at the park and a few hours reprieve from grief. Apparently for me, too.

A park photographer clicked off a few shots of the cast members dancing with audience members and then the Bride of Frankenstein approached him, beaming twins tethered to each hand.

She smiled beguilingly as she held out a coupon. "Stop at the picture kiosk on your way out and pick up a souvenir picture." Her hand touched his as he accepted the slip of paper.

Patrick's heart actually fluttered in his chest. "Thank you. We will."

One more heart-piercing smile and she danced her way back up onto the stage. A few minutes later, she took her last bow and shimmied out of sight amid the boom and sputter of fireworks that curtained the stage with smoke.

He stood for a moment hoping to catch one more glimpse, but all that remained on stage was a dry ice haze and the gunpowder odor of spent pyrotechnics. Clasping the girls by the hand, he climbed the steps out into blazing sunshine.

Squinting and perspiring again, he led them toward the park exit, stopping at the photo booth and handing over the identifying coupon.

"Why did you buy three, Uncle Pat?" Peggy asked as she pushed through the turnstile.

"I bought an extra just in case your mom wants it," he fibbed, a souvenir of the Graveyard Revue earmarked for him.

****

Quiet during the car ride to the western Chicago suburb, the girls were undoubtedly worn out from their day in the sunshine. Checking the mirror to view the backseat, each stared out the window, their faces slack. No way to prevent the reality of missing their daddy to settle back into little bones.

Surprised to see his brothers half-heartedly tossing a basketball around in Kay's driveway, Patrick drove over the opposite apron into the circular drive. The girls perked up and jumped out of the car as soon as Patrick stopped. Turning the ignition off, he slid out of the car.

"Uncle Danny, guess what? We got picked to go up on stage and dance with the Bride of Frankenstein and we have a picture. Want to see it?" Amanda hurried over to her godfather, the plastic bag containing her picture dangling from her hand.

"You bet I want to see it. Aunt Molly is inside. Let's go show her, too."

"Do you have a picture?" Joe passed the ball to Brian and knelt down in front of Peggy.

"I do, too, Uncle Joe. Is Aunt Bobbie here?"

"Sure is, honey. She's inside feeding Emma."

"Oh boy. Maybe she'll let me help." Peggy ran towards the open front door, Joe tailing her.

"How'd it go?" Brian asked, after Joe had closed the door.

"They had a great time. The Graveyard Revue was the biggest hit of the day. They knew every word to every song."

"That was my favorite part of the day, too, when I took them. How about that Bride of Frankenstein? Wasn't she something? Wow. That short skirt and leather thing she wore, all that black spiky hair, the huge bedroom eyes..."

"The fiancée you have?"

Brian arched his eyebrows. "I know, but I can still look can't I?"

Patrick snorted. "The Bride of Frankenstein we saw had long, curly black hair."

"They must have more than one actress for the part. Too bad you missed the one I saw. She was really something." Brian casually bounced the ball in front of him.

"How were things around here today?" Patrick asked, his voice low.

"Not too bad. You just missed Mom and Pop. They left to stay at Danny and Molly's condo downtown to give Kay a little alone time with the kids tonight. Kay only baked three lemon pound cakes, two coconut custard pies and one pumpkin bread, so I think she's feeling better."

Patrick shook his head. "This sure sucks."

"You got that right."

The door opened. Danny and Joe loped toward them.

"Are you staying for dinner, Pat? Maybe we'll grab some Chinese takeout, then head home," Brian suggested.

"Wish I could, but I have to get back to my desk for a while tonight."

"How's the new job going?" Danny inquired.

"Uphill but improving. Really feeling the effect of CPD lay-offs in the department."

"I hear ya," Joe declared. "Sorry you turned down that job at ATF now, Captain?"

Patrick flicked his eyes toward Kay's house. *I want...no I need to be close to my family.* "Glad I didn't move out of state then, and especially now. I'll get my arms around this new job. A case goes to trial Monday and I want to review the file."

"You're testifying?" Joe asked, his tone insinuating surprise.

"No, just observing, but I need to be prepared."

Joe nodded. "Who's the defense attorney?"

"C. J. Demarco. Ever hear of him?"

Danny laughed. "You're in for it. Charlie Demarco is a real ball buster."

Joe apparently thought something was mighty funny, too, as he rolled his eye in Danny's direction. "Make sure you have every t crossed and i dotted.

K. M. Daughters

Even the slightest mistake and you won't know what hit you."

Patrick contemplated the goofy expressions on his three brothers' faces. "Something you guys want to tell me?"

Brian patted his back. "Good luck, bro. You'll need it."

Chapter 2

In contrast to the summer-like weekend, temps today hovered in the mid fifties. Rain pounded the roof of the squad car, streaming in blanketing sheets down the windshield while the wipers feebly batted the deluge. Monday morning traffic on Lake Shore Drive crawled, a parade of frustration for Patrick. Stiff and formal clad in his new uniform, captain's bars on its sleeve, he merged onto the Stevenson Expressway due only to the good graces of a driver who came to a dead halt for a CPD squad car.

Expressway, my ass. Tempting, but he'd resist riding the shoulder, blue lights swirling to clear a path, never one to abuse the official use of police power. Court wouldn't convene for another forty-five minutes and he was auditing the proceedings in the inherited case anyway.

Exiting at Damen after a long stint of riding the brakes, Patrick drove toward the main criminal justice court building on south California, half-listening to dispatch squawk. When he pulled up, a couple of parking spaces remained. Out of the car in the downpour, he sprinted toward the entrance, fifteen minutes past the scheduled court time.

Easing through the courtroom's doors, Patrick chose a seat in the back row. Florescent lighting bleached the skin tones of those present an unnatural greenish-white and hummed faintly overhead. Seated at the table at the right front of the room, the defense players presented their backs to him. The defendant, Dominic Tonnelli, wore a gray pinstriped suit and sat erect, an unmoving stiff posture. To Tonnelli's left, the only other person seated at the table was a woman.

The formidable C. J. Demarco is a girl. Now the goofy expressions his brothers had worn when cautioning him on Saturday made sense to Patrick. *Could have provided more specifics, guys.*

The prosecutor finished questioning Sergeant Lucas, one of Patrick's men. Lucas' eyes scanned the courtroom and located Patrick. The sergeant acknowledged his superior with a quick nod of his head and Patrick returned the gesture.

Charlie Demarco rose from her seat slowly for the cross-exam. Glossy black hair knotted tightly in a bun low on the back of her neck. Tall and slim in a long beige suit jacket that covered her rear end and a skirt that covered the backs of her knees, she rounded the table corner and approached the witness stand on thin-heeled black pumps.

Something about the way she moves. Sinuous, graceful, like a dancer.

"Officer Lucas, you testified that an informant alerted you and your partner to the narcotics shipment confiscated from the industrial park warehouse on January twelfth this year. Did that informant also provide information implicating the defendant, Dominic Tonnelli, prior to January twelfth?" Her melodic voice sounded familiar.

"Yes," Lucas replied. "Word on the street."

"Word on the street." She rolled each syllable off her tongue in exaggerated enunciation, her flat tone implying that the statement was ridiculous. "Was the defendant present at the time of the raid?"

"No, only two of his mules."

"Your department has not established any association between the defendant and *his* so-called mules during testimony at either of their trials or via any other evidence. Isn't that correct, Sergeant?" Charlie leaned forward, a not so-subtle stance meant to intimidate.

"They wouldn't finger him." Lucas stared at her unblinking. "But he owns the building." He pointed at Tonnelli.

C. J. Demarco turned her back on Lucas and strode briskly, high heels clicking, to the defense table. Purple-blue eyes gleamed and her chin slightly jutted upward with a trace of confidence or conceit. A smile stretched on her closed lips, imparting an air of self-satisfaction. *She's sure a poised performer.*

Patrick sucked in a breath. The woman who had inspired serious consideration about hanging around backstage at The Graveyard Revue in the near future, extended a delicate hand down to finger papers spread on the defense table. Prim hair instead of those wild, blue-black curls and practically shapeless in that suit—there was still no mistaking her. A couple of interesting starring roles in Patrick's dreams later, the Bride of Frankenstein now appeared ready to take his sergeant apart.

Why the hell would one of the highest priced defense attorneys in the city moonlight as an amusement park singer? But it has to be her.

Dangling a sheet of paper in her right hand, Charlie strolled halfway back to the witness stand. "You ascertained that Mr. Tonnelli owns the warehouse in question. Is that correct, Sergeant?"

She stood, seemingly relaxed with her arms at her sides.

"The owner of record is Tuscan Imports," Lucas maintained bluntly, "And Dominic Tonnelli is the registered owner of that business."

"He is indeed the owner of Tuscan Imports." Charlie twisted her neck, facing the jury, her profile eye-catching. "To your knowledge have any illegal activities or allegations been associated with Tuscan Imports or Mr. Tonnelli personally before January twelfth of this year?"

"To my knowledge, he's as crooked as a drunk walking the line on New Year's Eve."

Ah shit.

"Move to strike!" Charlie faced the judge squarely.

"Strike that response." The judge addressed Lucas, "Sergeant. A simple yes or no."

Stiff-shouldered, Lucas glared in Charlie's direction. "No."

"For clarity, I'd like you to confirm the events preceding the raid one more time." Charlie raised her right hand holding the paper, glanced at it, and then let it dangle at her side again. "Based on an informant's tip, you moved to intercept a narcotics shipment bound for 3W4336 Industrial Boulevard on the night of January twelfth. When you arrived at the location were there any signs of illegal activity outside the building?"

Lucas' shoulders eased down an inch. "No. An empty cargo truck was parked in a back loading bay. My team surrounded the building and then entered from multiple locations."

"You obtained a signed warrant to search and seize the contents of the building."

Lucas squinted. "Yes. Woke the judge up in the middle of the night."

Charlie approached the stand, paper outstretched toward Lucas. "Please inspect this document carefully, Sergeant. Is this the search warrant you obtained?" She laid a hand on the wooden railing in front of Lucas.

Lucas accepted the paper, bent his head to scrutinize it. "Yes, it is."

"Are your signature and the signature of your supervisor present on the appropriate lines of the warrant?"

The back of Patrick's neck prickled.

Lucas raised his eyes from the paper. "Yes."

Leaving her hand on the railing, Charlie turned away from Lucas, facing the jury instead. "And the judge's signature is on the appropriate line, also?"

Lucas crooked a finger in the collar of his shirt before he bent his head over the warrant again.

Patrick's blood pressure spiked, pulse accelerating. *Damned well better be.*

"Yes," Lucas confirmed softly.

Patrick expelled a breath.

Charlie headed back toward Tonnelli, scooped another document off the table, reversed and carried it to the bench. "Judge, the defense requests that this title report be entered as Defense exhibit eight."

The judge flipped the pages and handed it back to her on a nod. Charlie transferred the document to Lucas. "Sergeant, please refer to the legal description on this title report and read aloud the title holder and the address referenced, please." She paced back to the table, skirted it and stood next to Tonnelli's seat, facing forward.

Lucas knit his brows and stared at her, his eyes slits, before he turned his attention to the document. "Title is held by Tuscan Imports, Limited," Lucas read. Dead silence while his eyes tracked back and forth. "The address is 3W4386 Industrial Boulevard."

"And the address on the search warrant aloud, please." Charlie drummed fingers on the tabletop.

Patrick imagined that his heart thumped along with his sergeant's, two drumbeats in the quiet courtroom.

Lucas stared at the warrant, his lips a grim line. His shoulders sagged and the response came, "3W4336 Industrial Boulevard."

"Motion for mistrial." Charlie's tone all business, matter-of-fact.

The gavel cracked like a gun discharging a

bullet aimed at Patrick's chest. "Motion granted. Case dismissed."

"Thank you, Judge." C. J. Demarco's voice as sweet as candy.

Shit, shit, shit. Patrick closed his eyes briefly, unable to ignore the annoying swell of chair scraping sounds and the overlapping comments of those around him. When he opened them again, C. J. Demarco stuffed papers in a briefcase and Lucas slumped in the witness stand staring at Patrick with a hangdog expression.

Tonnelli, on his feet, shook Demarco's hand once before beating it up the aisle past Patrick. His expensive suit, starched white shirt, power tie, and impeccably groomed silver hair befitted his still intact reputation as a kingpin above the law. Charlie followed her client up the aisle a minute later, broadly smiling, all long legs and lovely femininity. The total opposite of the icy barracuda she had seemed moments before.

Patrick's eyeballing her must have carried the intended heat because her smile dimmed before she glanced at him on the approach to the door. Her violet eyes danced as if her brain turned behind them to make the connection to the sight of his face. A subtle double take and recognition apparently flashed. Her eyes widened and she grinned, her head tilted just like it had on stage. As she sped toward him, Charlie tossed out, "Hey there, Uncle *Captain* Pat. Fancy meeting you here."

"Coldhearted on stage and off, Counselor."

Pausing in the aisle abreast of him, she locked violet eyes on his and replied, "Ouch."

She zipped through the doors, a flash of beige material and pretty, flexing calves atop high heels. With an exasperated sigh, Patrick stood and trudged toward the witness stand to mop up the mess with Lucas.

Chapter 3

Sunshine speared through dark clouds overhead. Charlie pushed through the main door of the building and faced a throng of reporters outside on the courtroom steps. Before the door closed behind her the press swarmed forward, brandishing network microphones like swords. A practiced serene smile creased Charlie's face. Using her soft leather briefcase as a shield, she shoved down the concrete stairs.

"How can you live with yourself?"

"What does it feel like knowing you got a drug lord off on a technicality?"

Charlie paused and drilled the young blonde reporter with a frigid stare. The blonde inched a step backward. "Maybe you should direct your question to Sergeant Lucas and his new CPD captain. Ask them how it feels to lose a case because of sloppy police work."

In motion, her for-the-cameras smile reinstalled on Charlie's face, shouted questions bombarded her like verbal bullets. "No comment," she replied.

A smile, a nod, another "No comment."

She continued down the stairs and the swarm shifted away, thinned. A quick glance over her shoulder at the figure emerging through the courthouse doors explained the path clearing before her.

Smiling widely, she reached the sidewalk unimpeded. *Uncle Pat with his shiny captain's bars gets his turn in the lion's den.*

Her suit jacket provided little protection against

the chilly breeze. She shivered, holding her lapels together with one hand as she hurried along the sidewalk. The cell phone clipped to the waistband of her skirt vibrated.

Juggling her briefcase, she slid the phone from its holder. "Demarco."

"Hey, CJ, congratulations."

"Thanks, Jamie. How did you hear already?" Halting at the intersection, Charlie waited for the traffic light to turn green.

"Good news travels fast."

A sleek limousine whizzed past her and rolled up to the curb.

"How about we celebrate your victory over lunch?"

"Sounds good. I'm headed back to the office. I'll pick up some sandwiches first and hail a cab."

"That's not what I had in mind."

Charlie turned her head toward the sound of a car horn. The back door of the parked car swung open and she smiled at the tall, tan man who emerged from the stretch limo clutching a cell phone to his ear.

Chuckling, Charlie shoved her phone back in its clip and walked toward him. "What exactly did you have in mind?"

Jamie snapped his cell phone shut and grinned. "Some burgers, some wine and a game of darts. I promise to let you beat me again."

Despite many distasteful things about working for Jamie Freemont, Charlie still had to appreciate his contagious zest for life. But he expected her to confine most of *her* waking life chained to a desk at his law firm.

Charlie shook her head. "My calendar is full, as usual, Jamie. I'll have to pass."

Jamie ignored her comment and punched a number into his cell phone. "Hi Carrie. C. J. has a lunch meeting and will be late getting back to the office. Just reschedule anything pressing. Thanks."

He gifted her with one of his sparkling smiles. "One of the neat perks of being the boss. Your assistant will handle your desk. Now about that lunch—how does The Jury Box sound?"

Playing hooky with permission. "It sounds perfect."

He took the briefcase out of her hand and tossed it in the back seat of the limo. "Take a lunch break, Johnny. We'll be across the street." Jamie pointed a finger toward the restaurant. "I'll call you when we're ready to be picked up."

The intersection cleared and Charlie strode next to him toward The Jury Box, a noisy pub and favorite hangout for both attorneys and police. A hostess led Jamie and Charlie to a prime booth near the dartboards. She slid into the bench across from him. After they placed their lunch orders, she leaned against the cushioned backrest and sighed, relaxed for the first time today. "This is nice. Thank you."

"You are so welcome. You earned it. I have to keep the shining star of Schotz, Pearson and Freemont happy." He reached across the table and squeezed her hand. "You are happy, aren't you?"

"Why wouldn't I be happy?"

He frowned and propped an elbow on the table, cupping his chin in his hand. "Hmm. Answering a question with a question, Counselor. Dodging perhaps? Everything okay with you?"

"Of course. Everything is great. I am very happy." Charlie posed, smiling as if Jamie held a camera. She wouldn't confess how truly unhappy she was to the only person who had generously supplied her a lifeline to grip while she untangled her messy life. He'd never understand how sick to her stomach it made her to free scum like Tonnelli and a parade of others based on technicalities or whatever means, never daring to delve into true innocence or guilt. But she needed the money and Schotz, Pearson and Freemont paid her plenty.

"Ready for a game?" Jamie pointed to the dartboard.

"Bring it on." Charlie slid out of the booth and grabbed a handful of darts. "Name your poison." She stood behind the throw line, ready to compete.

He glanced at the Rolex on his wrist. "We have time for a quick game of Around the Clock. Ladies first."

Charlie fired six darts in a row, dead on target. She would have nailed the seventh but caught movement of a massive shadow in the corner of her eye that drew her focus. Captain Uncle Pat lumbered over to the bar and settled his brawny self down on a stool. Back to her, his shoulders spanned a yard compared to a one-foot waist.

"Finally." Jamie took his place behind the throw line. "I didn't think you were going to give me a chance." He threw four darts before one missed the mark.

Conscious of Pat's attention, his eyes leveled on her bringing prickling heat, Charlie prepared to throw her next dart. Showtime again. After fourteen darts hit the mark, she turned her head toward the bar and gazed into his twinkling, azure eyes. He raised his coffee cup in a salute. An unexpected shimmer of pleasure coursed through her at the simple tribute.

Jamie's arm circled her waist and broke the moment. Leading her back to the booth he remarked, "You're even more deadly than I remembered."

The waitress brought a bottle of wine to the table. After Jamie completed the ceremony of opening and tasting, he raised his glass. "Congratulations, C. J. You did another fine job.

Keep those billable hours coming." He laughed. "You were great today. I am so proud of you."

"Thank you, Jamie. That means so much to me." She sipped her wine and glanced at the captain's reflection in the mirror behind the bar. *The new captain—my hot man in the audience.*

****

Patrick flicked his eyes away when she glanced at the mirror. It took every ounce of willpower he possessed to quit staring at the woman's reflection. He was drawn to C. J. Demarco like a cat to a saucer of warm milk. Or maybe the clueless fly to the cagey black widow.

Who is she? The sexy siren at the amusement park, the frigid unbeatable lawyer, the gunslinger at darts or the soft woman relaxing over a glass of wine?

In the mirror, their glasses clinked in the air, in obvious enjoyment. Probably celebrating the mistrial. Patrick sipped coffee, pissed off yet mildly jealous.

The woman on stage had lingered in his mind and he had considered how he might connect with a virtual fantasy. That was before the fantasy morphed into the infamous C. J. Demarco.

The man seated opposite her left the booth.

Patrick swiveled off the stool leaving his coffee mug on the bar, intent on connecting with the reality of this intriguing woman now seated in his world.

"Celebrating, Counselor?" He leaned against the booth, his hands deep in his pants pockets.

"As a matter of fact, I am celebrating, Captain." She beamed, a seemingly self-satisfied smile.

"Sit down." Charlie waved her hand at the bench opposite her.

"No, thanks. Your boyfriend might object."

"He won't mind."

Patrick slipped his hands out of his pockets and

sat on the bench, resting his forearms on the table.

"Would you like a glass of wine?" she inquired.

"No, thank you. I'm…"

The boyfriend stood a couple inches away from his elbow. Rising, Patrick muttered, "Here's your seat."

"Thanks." Taking a backward step, he squinted at Patrick. "Captain Sullivan, isn't it?" He extended a hand and Patrick clasped it in a handshake.

"That's right. I'm Patrick Sullivan."

"Good to meet you, Patrick. I'm Jamie Freemont with Schotz and Pearson. I heard you were promoted to CPD Captain. I've followed your career with the ATF."

"Have you now?"

Freemont smiled. "Yes. You did some great work cleaning up the streets."

"Thank you. I had a great team."

"Too bad it didn't go your way in court today."

The zinger delivered smooth as the well lubricated defense attorney he is.

Patrick refused to glance at Charlie and give her a chance to gloat, too. "It's more than too bad." Patrick shrugged, but he leveled a glare at Fremont.

Unperturbed by Patrick's expression, he gestured toward the booth. "Sit please. I'm sorry, C. J., I have to run. Pearson's son just got arrested at college for disorderly conduct. He doesn't even call his father anymore. Has me on speed dial. I have to go get the little punk out."

"Anything I can do to help?" Charlie regarded Fremont with upturned eyes, a stunning light purple color the likes of which Patrick had never seen before his visit to the amusement park.

"No. I'll handle it and make a few calls to clear the brat. Take the rest of the day off. You deserve it. Enjoy your lunch. Nice to meet you, Captain. Take good care of my girl."

"Yeah, sure." Patrick sat, watching Fremont leave, "my girl" ringing in his ears.

"My boss, not my boyfriend." Charlie broke the silence.

"I didn't ask."

"No, but you were wondering."

"You have no idea what I'm thinking," he replied.

"Why don't you tell me then?" She leaned back, folding her arms across her chest.

Patrick folded his arms, too, leaning against the table's edge. "You work for the most prestigious law firm in Illinois. Why do you moonlight in the Graveyard Rock N Roll Revue?"

"I'm an exhibitionist." Straight faced, amusement danced in her eyes.

Charlie snorted and then she burst out laughing. "If you could see your face right now. I'm kidding. I was just helping someone out. It's fun. An escape. It's a lot easier than my day job."

"Speaking of your day job." Patrick pointed to the dartboards where his sergeant aggressively heaved a dart into the bulls-eye. "How much do you want to bet that Lucas over there is imagining your picture on that board?"

Charlie shrugged her shoulders. "Not my fault your side lost. His sloppiness was his downfall. He can't blame me." Her fingers stroked the stem of her wine glass.

Patrick's elbows dug into the tabletop. "Of course he can. A two-year case went down the toilet because of a typo."

She shook her head. "I wasn't doing the typing."

Annoyed, he concluded, "You are tough."

"I am not going to deny that." Something flickered in her eyes. *Regret?* "I have to be tough to do my job."

Me, too. "Incompetent paperwork won't happen

again on my watch."

Her eyes hardened, an unyielding expression. "If it does, trust me, I'll catch it."

The waitress propped a huge tray of food on the edge of the table and dealt plates along its surface like cards.

"I'll leave you to your meal," Patrick remarked.

"We must have been very hungry when we ordered. Can't let it go to waste. Help yourself." Charlie dug into a rare burger with gusto, blood-tinged juices leaking onto her hands. Patrick's stomach clenched. *Damn, she's hot. And I skipped breakfast.*

Her hand brushed his as they both reached for an onion ring. Fire shot up his arm. The blast of lust made him hunger for a taste of her—not the charred meat on his plate. His burger lay untouched in front of him. Hers completely vanished.

"Something wrong with the burger?" Charlie crunched on an overcooked French fry.

"Do you want it?"

"No, I couldn't." She stared at the burger a second and then snatched it off his plate. "Maybe just a taste."

Biting off a quarter of the burger, she set it back on his plate, chewed, swallowed, finished off her glass of wine and sat back with a contented sigh.

Amused, Patrick declared, "Impressive. Where do you put it?"

Charlie dabbed her mouth with a napkin. *Very sensual.*

"I have a very fast metabolism," she related. "My sister hates me. I can eat anything I want and never gain a pound. She teases that she looks at what I eat and gains weight."

Interested in this semi-human side of her, Patrick probed, "You close to her?"

"She's my best friend. How about you? Any

sisters?"

"One sister and four brothers." The memory of Jimmy constricted Pat's chest. He didn't rephrase and qualify the sibling count at three *living* brothers, one killed in the line.

"Big family. Are you close?"

"Definitely. My brothers are my best friends." *Who I'm going to beat senseless for not telling me more about you, lady.*

"That's wonderful. I know how precious that is." A sweet smile and her eyes softened.

Drawn to the enigma she presented, he'd delay returning to work. "How about a game of darts to wear off some of that food?" He'd beat her at one game and then head to the station house.

"Sounds good to me."

Shrugging out of her suit jacket and tossing it on her seat, Charlie lost the who-goes-first round and Patrick threw the first dart. The gardenia scent of her perfume distracted him and his second dart missed its mark.

She ran off eight before her ninth missed by a hair. Determined to focus on the sport rather than the hints of lingerie beneath Charlie's sleeveless silk blouse, Patrick shot off eleven straight taking the advantage. He relinquished it to Charlie, won it, back and forth until she won the match.

"Seems to be my lucky day today." With a bratty grin, she turned toward the booth.

He wanted to kiss that bratty grin off her face, but could finish the loser if he took that route, too. "Somehow I don't think luck has anything to do with it."

Following behind her, he appreciated the graceful sway of her hips. Patrick stood leaning against the table as Charlie slid onto the bench.

Patrick flagged the waitress over with a wave of his hand. She brought a bill folder to the table. He and Charlie reached for it at the same time.

"It's a receipt." The waitress handed the vinyl folder to Charlie. "The gentleman paid before he left."

"That was nice," he commented sarcastically.

"Jamie is a great guy."

Patrick raised his eyebrows.

Charlie chuckled. "I told you Jamie is my boss not my boyfriend."

His phone vibrated in his pocket. He fished it out and checked the text message. "I have to go."

"I have to get back to the office, too."

"Your boss gave you the afternoon off." Patrick held her jacket for her and slipped it up over her shoulders, his fingers skimming along the petal soft skin of her arms.

She shivered at his touch, triggering Patrick's impulse to caress more fully, make her tremble all over.

His phone vibrated again in his hand.

"Better get that. See ya, Pat." She stood on tiptoe and kissed his cheek, her flowery nearness tempting him to toss the vibrating phone away and pull hairpins out of the bun at the back of her neck.

But Charlie already moved away from Patrick. The phone tickled his palm as he watched her strut out the front door of The Jury Box.

He slowed the car to a crawl, inching up on the woman in a skirt that just covered her ass, maintaining a rapid, wobbly gait on stiletto heels. He shook off the dim memory of wobbling on his mother's high heels in her closet and the sting of the back of his father's hand across his face.

Pulling alongside her, he said, "You working?"

Turning her head without slowing down, her eyes widened, but her reply sounded bored. "Depends on the job."

"Nothing kinky." Keeping pace next to her, he picked up a few hundred-dollar bills and fanned them in an upraised hand.

When she halted, he braked, smiling at her approach to his car.

"What do you have in mind? Nice ride."

"Five hundred to do me in the car. A hundred to hand me your panties while I drive us someplace a little more private."

"I'm definitely working." She swung the car door open and plopped down on the passenger seat. "Let's have that first bill."

He waved the hundred-dollar bills back and forth before he shifted gears with the same hand and gunned the engine. "Panties first."

Speeding toward the alley he had scoped out, she shimmied in the passenger seat and emitted a little grunt.

Chapter 4

With a couple months into the new job under his belt, Patrick's confidence measured about medium on his personal meter to handle whatever the press threw his way at the superintendent's scheduled conference. Proud of his record at ATF and the distinction of being the youngest captain on the force, Patrick prepared to take questions at the mic after the super's glowing introduction.

"It's my pleasure to introduce Captain Patrick Sullivan, who will now take your questions." Superintendent O'Halloran squeezed back toward the American and CPD flags and the backdrop photo of the Chicago cityscape at the rear of the cramped podium.

Patrick shook his superior's hand and then turned toward the lectern facing the assembly seated on rows of folding chairs. "Good morning, ladies and gentlemen."

"Did you suspend Sergeant Lucas from active duty after the Tonnelli trial yesterday?" came the gruff shout from a husky, middle-aged guy in the back of the room. Patrick didn't recognize him.

Meeting the man's eyes Patrick replied, "No, sir, I did not."

Purposefully shifting his gaze to the raised hand of a woman in the front row, "Ma'am?"

"Did you reprimand him?" the guy in the back persisted.

"No. It's not my style and he doesn't deserve a reprimand in my opinion." Patrick hadn't taken his eyes off the lady in the front, encouraging her now to speak.

"Captain, are the cutbacks..."

"Don't you think a reprimand is in order?" The same pain in the ass cut off the woman in mid-sentence.

"What is your name, sir?" Patrick posed in a pleasant tone, focusing on the rude guy.

"Harry Mitchell."

"Mr. Mitchell, despite the disappointing outcome of the trial, Sergeant Lucas and his partner, Officer Garcia headed an operation that removed illegal drugs with a three million dollar street value from the system. I think you'll all agree that doesn't deserve a reprimand." Patrick smiled at the woman in the front row. "Miss?"

"Captain, are the recent cutbacks responsible for the failure of your department to apprehend the serial killer at large?" She poised her fingers over a small computer keyboard balanced on her knees.

Patrick's stomach dove. "Cutbacks have nothing to do..."

The barrage fired from all quadrants like a spray from a machine gun.

"Can you confirm the number of victims at five?"

"Method of death is strangling?"

"All prostitutes, right? Left with trash in alleys by the same killer? The Garbage Man Murderer?"

"Can you verify accounts that rape is involved?"

Shit, I have leaks to contend with? Patrick stared straight ahead, mic beneath his chin with his hand upturned, palm forward. "Ladies and gentlemen, kindly allow me to respond," he boomed.

Papers rustled, a cough and then blessed silence. Patrick scanned the room, noted the hawkish expressions on the reporters' faces. He waited a beat before speaking, a device to temper his remarks, suppress frustration and establish authority.

"Thank you. First, I'll address cutbacks." He paused. "We regret that Chicago, like other great cities in the country, has budget deficits and cutbacks are unavoidable. However, I assure you they have not had and will not have a negative impact on the department's ability to protect the citizens of this city. To the last man, my department is proud to serve."

Several hands waved in the audience. Patrick ignored them and continued, his calm voice belying his steadily increasing pulse. "The recent murders of five victims appear to be connected, and an aggressive investigation of these crimes is underway. The victims were all strangled and their bodies were discovered in deserted alleys in five different locations. Assaults of a sexual nature were also involved. As you know, no one has yet stepped forward with information leading to an arrest."

Superintendent O'Halloran tapped Patrick's shoulder. He turned his head and stepped aside when O'Halloran jutted his head forward toward the mic. "That's all for today, folks," O'Halloran declared. On a handshake, still hovering over the mic, the super added, "Thanks for taking the time to be here, Captain Sullivan."

****

Not the ideal way to start a workday, but Patrick accepted that the whole spokesman thing came with the territory. Pleased with his overall handling of the questions surrounding Tonnelli's mistrial, the image of Charlie firing darts flashed through his mind. Right now he needed to keep his mind off the woman—a seemingly impossible feat lately. *Later, I'll focus on the way to get her out of my head permanently.*

Patrick swept into the station house on a bead for his lieutenant's desk to confer with him about the five victims, murder board locked away in his office.

He detoured after the snap decision to introduce himself to the district's new profiler. The recent summary of the Garbage Man Murders he had provided at the press conference replaced Charlie Demarco in his mind's replay.

Patrick glimpsed stacked boxes lined on the floor through the open office door. A man with longish black hair streaked with a couple strands of white-gray bent over an open box in the center of his desk. Rapping on the doorframe, he asked, "Got a minute?"

"Sure. C'mon in, Captain." He turned keen, green eyes bordered by laugh lines in Patrick's direction, his arm outstretched over the lid of the box.

Patrick clasped his hand and shook it. "Pat Sullivan. Nice to meet you, Captain Dowd."

"It's Flynn, Pat. Have a seat if you don't mind using one of those boxes." His eyes dipped down toward the mess on his floor.

"If you have time to consult on a case, we can grab some coffee and talk in the conference room."

"I'll make time." Flynn skirted the desk.

On the way to the coffee maker, Patrick said, "I advised Tom Gable to send you the file on the investigation he's leading. The serial killer. Have you had a chance to look at it?"

"The Garbage Man Murderer?" Dowd kept pace with his strides.

"That's the one," Pat replied, sick and tired of the catch phrases the media so loved.

"Oh yeah." Flynn poured a mug of coffee at the machine, filled another for Patrick and handed it to him. "I haven't had time to write my report. Want me to just talk through some of my impressions?"

"Yes. Let's pull Gable into the conference room and have him bring in the murder board as a reference." He showed Flynn to the door of the conference room. "Have a seat. I'll be right back."

Patrick strode away and rubbernecking over cubicle walls, spied Gable seated at his desk. "Hey, Tom," he called. "Bring the board into the conference room for a minute?" He tossed Tom the keys to his office.

Reversing, Patrick joined Flynn at the conference table and took a couple sips from the coffee mug while he waited for Gable to prop the murder board up on the end of the table and take a seat.

Flynn squinted at the board, shook his head several times. "Let me just ramble a while, okay?"

Patrick nodded.

"COD in all five cases is strangulation. Very intimate, personal. Your killer is strong— undoubtedly male. Autopsies show facial bruising of victims on one or both cheeks. He punches them in the face. Stuns them into submission. No sign of struggle for any of the victims. He immobilizes them with a punch or punches and completely overpowers them. Suffocates them to death with his hands around their necks. Takes strength, takes a huge amount of rage, and takes time. No turning back for this guy when their faces turn blue. His rage is focused on overpowering, controlling, leaving no room for opposition. Whatever he thinks these women did to deserve this, there is no question he thinks a face to face painful death is what they have coming. Women have emasculated this guy. Could be his mother. Could be a girlfriend that serves as the model he's killing over and over. Maybe his mother or girlfriend were or are prostitutes. Or, if Mom cheated on Dad or the girlfriend cheated on him, he might consider that an act of prostitution. Symbolically, he could be victimizing prostitutes. The garbage tags should be taken literally. His opinion of these women."

"What about the bats?" Patrick interjected.

"Excellent question." Flynn stood and walked closer to the murder board. Pausing on each crime scene photo with respectful attention to each victim, he continued, "The post mortem brutality adds another strong psychological element. They're already dead, but he's not done with them. He rams a baseball bat up inside them. Picture the violence necessary to create those photographs up here. Beyond rage. Nothing sexual about these acts. However, it has everything to do with sexuality. His sexuality. The bat as the ultimate phallus. Your killer has serious conflicts with his own masculinity, his own adequacy and he's furious about it. The rage is all directed at females, specifically females whom men pay for sexual acts. Your perp may be sexually conflicted, although that's not a strong impression. One thing for sure, either he thinks or he knows his penis doesn't measure up, at least symbolically. And chances are a female gets the blame for enforcing that perception. Your killer is proverbially or possibly literally under-hung."

Gable snorted.

Patrick huffed a breath. "That an official psychological term?"

Flynn grinned at him. "Off the cuff. I'll clean it up for the report I submit."

"Thanks for the input, Flynn." Patrick stood. "Tom, come with me and let's lock up that board."

Gable followed him into his office and covered the board.

Patrick rounded the edge of his desk and faced the credenza behind it. An array of framed family photos monopolized most of the space on the cherry veneer surface—the most recent addition the twins with the Bride of Frankenstein. Her image prompted a sexual tug in the pit of his stomach. *Too bad you turned out to be C. J. Demarco, Bride.*

He rolled his chair back and sat behind his desk.

Gable occupied a chair in front of the desk. "We've still got nothing on this sick bastard."

"Pretty much," Patrick admitted. No prints, no DNA traces, what they needed was somebody who could figure out the last john in common for the five victims. "Have we found anything at all that ties the victims besides this lunatic's MO?"

"Not a damn thing."

"Can we tie them to the same pimp?"

"We brought Vice in on it months ago," Gable replied. "So far it looks like these women operated solo. Five out of five have been picked up before for soliciting from all over the city grid. Last residences of record are all over the map, too. If there's a common thread, damned if I can find it."

Patrick sighed. "All right. See if you can round up some men to keep up the canvassing. Somebody had to see something in five different vicinities. Let me know if *anything* turns up."

"Yes, sir."

Chapter 5

The mist blanketing the water below glittered silver as the sun rose over Lake Michigan. Charlie gazed through the sliding glass doors leading to the wraparound balcony off her bedroom suite. Sipping steaming lemon tea from an oversized mug, she luxuriated in the solitude. Lazy mornings when she could spend a few minutes enjoying the amazing sunrise view from her condo in the sky didn't usually fit into her insane work schedule. Her temporary home, a prime piece of high-rise real estate situated on the prestigious Lake Shore Drive, offered a view of Lake Michigan on one side and the remarkable view down into Wrigley field on the other. Too bad she was a Sox girl, mostly to aggravate her boss.

C. J. Demarco didn't have to be in court until noon today. On days like this, Charlie normally started her office day before six, churning out billable hours until leaving at the last minute for a pre-court client conference or to take her place behind the defense table. She had an army of junior associates and researchers at the firm, but she rarely delegated. Today really was no less pressing than her typical workday, but she hadn't spent any time with Emily in over a week and she missed her sister. *This morning nothing's more important to me than sister time.*

A knock on the door turned Charlie away from the glittering lake. "Are you up?" came Emily's muffled voice.

"Come on in."

Emily barreled through the door, black hair

spiking in all directions, mascara streaks under her eyes. "I got your note last night when I got in. I've missed talking to you, too. This is great."

Charlie smiled into the mirror image of her own dark lavender eyes, practically an identical reflection in every way, yet as opposite as two people could be. Charlie required neatness in her personal haven; everything had a place. The clothes in her closet hung organized by style and color. Shoes lined up in military precision like soldiers in review formation.

Venturing into Emily's room, two doors down the hall, the first instinct would be to call the police and report a burglary. Clothes draped the bed and floor, drawers hung open, and clutter overflowed every available flat surface. Charlie couldn't live amid such chaos, so by unspoken decree, they spent most of their down time together in Charlie's room, a tranquil oasis.

Emily held up a bakery bag. "I thought we needed some celebratory scones. Congratulations on winning another case."

Her back against the cool glass door, Charlie grinned. "Oh thanks. More important, I'm dying to know. Have you heard anything about the audition?"

"Nothing yet. But I think I nailed it. I'm keeping my fingers crossed for a callback. Thanks again for covering for me." Emily leaped into a landing on the middle of Charlie's bed, precariously sloshing coffee through the slit cap of her *venti* cup.

"It's the least I can do," Charlie admitted, eyeing her bedspread.

Plunging a hand in and out of the bag, Emily heaped scones on a napkin, her eyes tracking Charlie's movements toward her.

Charlie selected a chocolate chip scone off the pile, sat and leaned against the headboard of her king-sized bed. Nibbling a corner of the buttery treat, she held Emily's stare. "What?"

"You have to stop blaming yourself." Emily broke off a piece of her scone aggressively and a cinnamon scent filled the room.

"Easier said than done," Charlie replied ruefully.

"Come on, Charlie. Look at us. We're living in this mind-blowing condo perched in the clouds."

"Thanks to a perk from my golden handcuffs—Schotz, Pearson and Freemont," she retorted sarcastically.

"No. Thanks to you. You earned the job. It wasn't handed to you. Give yourself some credit."

"Look what I did to Mom and Dad. I'll never forgive myself for what I've put them through."

Emily's eyes darkened. "You didn't do anything to them. Giovanni did. He's responsible, not you. They know that."

"But I brought him into their lives. If I hadn't fallen…" Tears welled and a lump in Charlie's throat prevented her from continuing.

Emily clasped Charlie's hands and squeezed them hard, eyes wide. "The only person who blames you for all that has happened is you. You have to forgive yourself."

"I won't forgive myself until I have repaid all the money Mom and Dad lost."

Suave, handsome, a foreign accent that made her toes curl, Giovanni had wooed, won and destroyed Charlie in only a year. Their accidental meeting at a charity fundraiser she had sponsored was anything but accidental in retrospect. He had taken aim at his target, Charlie, and had swept her off her feet. Bull's eye. So charming, attentive, deceptive and lethal to her self-esteem. She had introduced him to her family and friends because she had trusted him.

Who else can I blame for the mess but me? "I

intend to replenish their retirement fund to the penny." Charlie huffed a sigh, a useless attempt to banish the ache near her heart. "I can't stand that they have to work at the grocery store now."

"Are you kidding? Dad loves his job. He gets to talk to all the customers." Emily swallowed the last bit of her scone and picked up another. "So does Mom."

"Still..." Despite the raw ache in her center, Charlie smiled at the thought of her parents. *They're so optimistic and energetic. And they do love working together, seeing neighbors regularly. But I destroyed their plans.*

"You know Mom and Dad never complain, but they don't deserve this. It breaks my heart to see all they had to give up because of that bastard. They should be playing golf with no responsibilities. I can't stand that this happened to them." Charlie got up and paced around her bedroom.

The morning sun blazed through the glass. She yanked the cord of the window blind and closed it, throwing the room into shadows.

"None of us can stand that Giovanni got away with this, but someday he'll pay for what he did to good people." Before Charlie had a chance to contradict her, Emily continued. "Now enough about you, let's talk about me."

Emily patted the bed with her hand, inviting Charlie to rejoin her. When she did, Emily pressed a finger over Charlie's lips. "Don't say one word about my giving up the thrilling life near Broadway to move to Chicago. I've found so many more opportunities here than I would ever have been offered in New York. And even better, I get to live in the lap of luxury with my best friend in the world. I have no complaints. And I have been saving the best for last." She dipped her chin, upturned eyes gleaming. "I might have a chance to audition for the lead in *Parkview Life.*"

"You're *kidding*." Charlie grabbed Emily's hand, thrilled at the possibility.

"Would I kid about something like that? Jamie called last night."

"Jamie as in Jamie Freemont? My boss?"

"Yep. I've talked to him a few times. Do you have a problem with that?"

"Not at all. I'm just surprised. He never mentioned talking to you when we had lunch the other day."

"It's no big deal. We aren't dating or anything. But I wouldn't say no if he asked me out on a date and I think he is getting around to asking. Anyway, he knows someone who knows someone who told him that Krista Martin is about to drop out as the lead in *Parkview Life.* He's going to give the producer my name. This could be *it*." Emily's voice rose, brimming with excitement. "This could be the big break I've been waiting for and it would never have been possible if I hadn't moved to Chicago with you. So you see? Everything is coming up Emily."

Charlie laughed. *It's impossible to resist Emily's top of the world attitude.* "It would be amazing if you get that part." Charlie closed her eyes. "You're perfect for it. I can see you up on that stage."

A smile curled her lips as she opened her eyes. Emily regarded her quizzically. "Remember when we saw the play last month? What did I say to you on the way out?"

"You said I would be better in that part than Krista."

"But you didn't believe me. See? The older sister is always right."

"Just three minutes older. I'll remind you when you turn forty before me." Emily chuckled. "I can't believe we polished off that whole bag of scones."

"We?" Charlie nibbled on her mostly intact

pastry.

Emily crumpled the bag in a lumpy ball and threw it towards the wastepaper basket, missing it by a mile. "So tell me a little about the new police chief."

"Why would I know anything about the new police chief?" Charlie sipped her tea, eyeing Emily over the rim of her mug.

"Haven't you watched the news? You've been on every channel for days. Everyone is talking about how you exposed the inept police force single-handedly."

"That's just crazy. I took advantage of a typo that's all. And I think you mean police captain."

"According to channel five you made a fool out of the new police...whatever *and* his squad and he has it out for you."

"That's ridiculous. I had lunch with Uncle Pat after the trial and it was very civilized," Charlie replied casually.

"Who's Uncle Pat? Lunch? You? What about the police chief? Hold that thought." Emily jumped off the bed and dashed out of the bedroom.

Kitchen cabinet doors banged and crackling noises sounded. Thud, thud, thud and Emily slipped into view. Bounding through the bedroom door, she hurtled onto the bed with a sea surge effect on the mattress. She dangled an arm toward Charlie, an oversized bag of M & M's clutched in her hand. "This calls for chocolate. Okay, tell me everything about your lunch. Don't leave anything out."

Charlie waved off the candy offer and laughed at Emily when she stuffed a handful of chocolate in her mouth, chewed energetically and stared at her. *I love you with all my heart, Emi.*

"Not much to tell. I actually met Uncle Pat at the amusement park, playing you." Charlie frowned. "Playing you, playing the Bride. He was there with his two nieces."

"You lost me."

"Sorry. Uncle Pat is the new captain."

"Oh. He looks hot on television," Emily mumbled over a mouth full of candy.

Oh, what the hell. Who cares if it's six a.m.? Charlie grabbed the bag of candy, slack in Emily's hand, poured some into hers, and handed it back to Emily.

"He's better looking in person," Charlie tossed out.

Emily snorted.

"Anyway, I took his nieces up on the stage."

"The nieces? Why didn't you take him up on the stage? I try to get all the hotties up to dance with me. One of the few benefits of the job." Her eyebrows arched and fell.

"I tried, but he refused. You can't imagine how shocked I was to see him in full uniform in the courtroom. I almost forgot why I was there. I think he was as surprised as I was. I ran into him again at The Jury Box. Jamie took me there for lunch but had to leave for a client. Pat came over to the booth just as Jamie was leaving. I couldn't let the food go to waste."

"Of course not." Emily smirked.

"So I invited him to share lunch. Beat him at darts. Gave him a kiss and left. End of story."

"A kiss?" Emily's mouth hung open. She clasped her chest in a pretend heart attack. "You kissed him?"

"A peck on the cheek and a goodbye"

"Are you going to see him again?" Emily smiled as Charlie hesitated.

"I'm sure I'll see him in court sometime."

"I'm not talking about C. J. Demarco, lawyer extraordinaire."

"I know what you're talking about. But no way."

"If he asked you out, would you go?" Emily leaned toward her, an impish expression on her face.

"It'll never happen." Charlie scowled, surprised at the pinch of disappointment from her own conclusion. "He called me a coldhearted bitch."

"Really?"

"Technically, he left out 'bitch,' but it was implied. He won't call socially."

"Oh, he'll call," Emily declared and then she sprinkled out a palm full of candy, stuffed it in her mouth.

"Is there anything I can do to help you get ready for your audition? "

"Changing the subject?"

"Definitely."

"I could use some help with the duet 'After Tonight.' I left the sheet music on the piano." Emily unfurled long legs and popped off the bed. "I probably should change my clothes."

Charlie followed her into the hallway. Emily sprinted into her bedroom at the sound of a cell phone trill. She smiled as Emily's laughter echoed in their home, Charlie's favorite music. What would she ever do without her sister? Ahead, a majestic baby grand piano occupied the corner of the glass-enclosed living room.

At the piano, Charlie focused on the sheet music, poised her fingers over the keys and hummed the tune as she played the melody line with her right hand. Then she softly sang, *"After tonight, will you still love me? After I have given my heart."*

She rested a hand on smooth ivory and gazed through the window bank, the vista a blur. Would she ever be able to give her heart again? The first man she had truly trusted with her heart had crushed it in his hands. Made an utter fool of her. Worse, her love affair hurt the people she loved most. Could she ever trust again?

Her thoughts turned involuntarily to the upstanding and downright outstanding Captain Sullivan.

"After I have given my heart," Charlie sang a cappella, her gaze scanning a wide arc over buildings and streets, part of Captain Sullivan's jurisdiction.

Chapter 6

Patrick made a fist and chopped down in the center of the barricade of crime scene tape that blocked his way. The webbing gave sufficiently for him to straddle it and stride toward the group of uniforms milling in the alley. The rancid stench of garbage and sour ammonia of urine pinched his nostrils.

He advanced in the pre-sunrise darkness toward the men, their silhouettes eerily glowing from reflected portable lighting set up on the ground. A few heads turned. "Morning, Captain," Gable greeted him.

"Morning, Tom. What can you tell me?" Patrick glanced down at the female corpse spread partially on the pavement, her upper torso propped up by a bed of plastic garbage bags dumped alongside the alley's brick wall.

"Same perp looks like." Tom's voice gruff. "Confirmed strangulation. TOD around three-thirty a.m. The usual violation."

The ME squatted over the body, haloed by a circle of halogen light. Patrick grimaced, noting the thick end of a baseball bat protruding from the victim's body. *Sick bastard.*

Tom's monotone cut through. "No victim ID, yet. Fucking makeshift garbage sticker around her toe." Tom wagged his head, eyes cast upward in disgust. "If he'd use a real garbage sticker maybe, just maybe we could trace something."

Patrick nodded. "Stickers are only used in the suburbs. As if our city district wasn't large enough a

46

challenge to throw a net over this guy." Dragging a hand through still shower damp hair, he glanced at the body. "A hooker again?"

"Can't know for sure until we have ID." Tom's eyes met his, sleep creases on the detective's face. "Dressed like one." He guffawed. "But so are Brittany Spears wannabes."

Patrick huffed a laugh. "Need me for anything?"

"Nah," Tom replied. "We'll start canvassing at a decent hour."

Patrick checked his watch. Four-thirty. "How'd you find her?"

"Sanitation guy starting his route." Tom pointed to a figure seated on the ground just beyond the perimeter of light. "We've pumped three cups of coffee into him and the poor guy is still shaking like he was electrocuted."

"Okay. I'm off duty today, but I'll be in the area if you need anything. No comment to the media." Patrick twisted his neck, scanning the mouth of the alley, turned back and peered toward the other open end. "Piece of luck the network vans aren't around."

"I guess." Tom rubbed a hand over his brown crew cut. "They'll be here soon enough I figure."

"Check in with me later."

Tom nodded and Patrick loped toward the alley entrance he'd used, hurdled the tape and ambled to his car. Disturbed, his mind spun, analyzing the scanty evidence and the means to implement an investigative strategy that would lead to solving the series of crimes. With a body count up to six, the horrific murder spree had to end.

Opening his car door, Patrick sat behind the wheel, turned the ignition key and waited for the ready light to switch on as the silent hybrid engine engaged. He'd left the squad car home assuming the scene visit would be his only on duty action today. Switching on the radio, he chose a smooth jazz station that broadcasted mostly mellow instrumentals. An upbeat sax number played on low volume as he drove along deserted streets, dissecting the case in his mind.

We've got to get ahead of this. Mount more foot and cruiser patrols during the times this guy hits. Do a roundup of prostitutes and get possible victims off the streets. Does he transport them by car to the dumpsites? Set up street barricades near alleys? Tomorrow I'll look at the scenes map again. See if that's feasible.

Regret over his new administrative role pinched his gut. *How do I launch a manhunt without squandering limited multi-department resources? I'll find the manpower somehow. But I could have an army and still be up against a wall on this.*

He slowed at the Clark and Hubbard intersection noticing the lights in the corner Starbucks. Rounding the corner, he parked, deciding to wait the ten minutes before the shop opened. The gas engine silenced as if the car stalled and the electric engine took over—something that had taken a while to grow accustomed to when Patrick had first driven the car.

Ebony black inside and out, it still had some sports car-like gleam to it and appealed to Patrick's male vanity—at least enough to satisfy him and surprising, also to attract the type of ladies he occasionally dated. Patrick preferred discerning women who looked beneath the surface and didn't mistake silence, in an engine or a man, as lack of fire within.

Charlie Demarco invaded his thoughts again. He'd yet to figure out how to prevent that. *Definitely not my type. Or is she?* Fired up just thinking about her, he remained baffled at his inability to control his mind.

The digital clock registered five and he swung

out of his car. Minutes later, Patrick drove toward Congress Street intending to park along the lakefront and enjoy his coffee while the sun rose over Lake Michigan. As if his car had a mind of its own, he turned west on Congress toward the Eisenhower extension away from the lake and toward the various Sullivan family residences.

Gathering speed as the city street became a highway, Patrick rode "home" toward the western suburbs. Strange that he had chosen to live in the city in adulthood. Half the family had migrated in the reverse. Danny, Kay, Joe and Brian had been born in a city hospital and raised crammed into an apartment. With the exception of Brian, his elder siblings had attended city elementary school until his parents saved enough to buy a rambling, money pit house in the suburbs. Patrick and Jimmy had been born and raised there.

Ironic. Jimmy's first apartment was in the city, too. For a while we were neighbors until he transferred to the burbs and was killed... Ah, Jimmy.

Now he knew why he had turned right instead of left on Congress. Patrick needed to spend some time with his only younger brother.

****

The cemetery gates opened daily precisely at six a.m.—Patrick's exact arrival time—as if he had planned the day off trip here to the minute. He steered along meandering, narrow lanes toward the crest of the hill where Jimmy Sullivan's gravestone marked his place of eternal rest. He parked at the remembered spot the hearse had occupied that freezing January day a little over a year ago when he had served as pallbearer at the side of Jimmy's casket. He trudged through the grass toward Jimmy's grave. Rows of pots held wilting Easter lilies, speckling the cemetery lawn with white dots. Another mourner stood with her head bent in the distance, acres away from him.

Patrick stopped when he reached the familiar spot. *James Francis Sullivan.* His baby brother's life reduced to a carving in a cold marble headstone. Running a calloused hand over the rough indentations on the top of the stone he swept away some dirt and grass clippings.

"Hey, kid." No need for silence or even whispers. No one could hear him. Maybe not even Jimmy.

"I'm working on a bitch of a case. Even your computer smarts couldn't help me crack this one."

Patrick surveyed the immaculate gravesite. Fresh flowers were arranged in an urn imbedded in the ground at the foot of the gravestone. He dipped a finger into the urn at the side of a cool, soft stem and hit water about an inch down. He smiled as he extracted his finger and wiped it along the outer seam of his jeans. "Mom is taking good care of things, huh, Jimmy?"

Or maybe it's Kay. "Has Kay been around lately, kid? Probably. Mike is buried over there somewhere."

Patrick raised his head and gazed toward the shimmering pond and the sprawl of geometric rows of varied grave markers. "I'll pay Mike a visit, too, if I can find his grave. Have you seen him? I'm counting on the two of you playing some ball up there and burning stuff on the barbecue grill."

Ah, Jimmy, I miss you, kid. "Who the hell can I beat up now in the family food chain?" Patrick smiled thinly, his heart aching. "Take care, Jim. I'll be back soon. I love you. Always did, always will."

Retracing his steps, Pat crossed the lane, bypassing his parked car. A breeze ruffled his close-cropped hair and the flower fragrant air helped to brace his sagging spirit. The landscape here was beautiful, peaceful, a haven from city noise and chaos. Eternal rest. Not a bad notion overall but damned depressing with lives as short as Jimmy's and Mike's, one brought down because of greed and the other because of a reckless driver. Senseless.

Crossing the lawn that blanketed the remains of other people, Patrick mused about what brought them to permanent rest. *Sickness, old age, violence?*

The latter possibility threw Patrick back into circular thinking about the Garbage Man Murderer. It was his job to prevent more grave digging, stop more permanent endings. Frustration and grief tore at him as if he had swallowed glass.

Patrick figured he headed in the right direction when he spied the slightly mounded earth of a fresh grave at the end of the row. The grave was marked with a temporary plaque flush with the ground. *Michael Joseph Lynch.* A tender blanket of grass seedlings had sprouted in the soil, so he stood on the neighboring grave to talk with Mike.

"Mike, she's destroyed by your death. I don't know how to help her. None of us do. We can hardly keep our heads above water. You are sorely missed." Patrick sighed, lifted his eyes toward the sky. An airplane engine droned and tree branches rustled.

"Molly says the hospital is falling apart without you. They can't seem to find a replacement to head up surgery. Ha. As if they could ever replace you."

Patrick squatted and leaned over the temporary marker crusted with dirt. His sister had shoved a flowerpot of tulips halfway down into the earth at the top of the plaque. Two round Mylar balloons on sticks with red hearts on the front and back were also "planted" on either side of Kay's flowers—a gift from the twins to their daddy, no doubt.

Maybe the innocence of Mike's little girls or the longing of a wife for her husband triggered the stabbing assault of grief. Patrick teetered in his squatting position and sat back on his haunches. Gulping air, he let the sadness fill him to do honor to the memory of two good men he would always love.

Sighing, he stood with downcast eyes. "I promise I'll look after your family. And keep them safe. Life is too damned short, isn't it, Mike? You made a difference and you'll always be remembered."

Patrick ambled back to the car amid the pretty scenery in the somber place. *If I were brought down in the line today...or hit by a bus, would I be remembered?* He liked to think that his career had made a small mark in his life's contribution book. Methodical, ambitious and resourceful he had strived to serve with honor. And as long as he wore the badge, he always would. Ruthless on the job, he was nearly the exact opposite off it. How many women had brushed him off because he was too nice?

Behind the wheel again, Patrick debated stopping at the station house and checking in with Joe and Brian. Or maybe a stop at Kay's? He could volunteer to drive the kids to school or nab whatever treat Kay might have handy in her "home bakery."

Driving aimlessly on familiar streets, he switched on the radio and punched the pre-set to a soft rock station.

One beat, two hearts. Two souls, one destiny... The male singer belted out the lyrics in sync with the pounding drums and electric guitar riffs. The dance worthy song lightened Patrick's mood, lost in the memory of the Bride of Frankenstein's velvety voice singing the same song, staring into his eyes.

Life is way too short. There must be a good reason why you're always in my head, Charlie.

Patrick pulled over to the curb and shoved the gearshift into park. After he obtained her office number with directory assistance, he dialed before he could reconsider.

"Schotz, Pearson and Freemont," came a sugary, female voice.

"Captain Patrick Sullivan for C. J. Demarco,

please."

"One moment, Captain."

Some classical hold music and a trip to her voice mail later, Patrick didn't regret the impulse to leave the message inviting Charlie to dinner.

More than pleased when the phone rang within five minutes, he answered, "Pat Sullivan," as he pulled to a curb again and let the engine idle.

"Pat, it's C. J. I got your message and I'm afraid I'll have to decline. Dinner will probably be something on the fly at my desk."

"That's too bad. Another evening, maybe?"

"I...no. I don't think so."

Her hesitation triggered a competitive response. "But you want to."

A sigh and white air.

"Look, Pat, I seriously doubt we're compatible."

"You'll never know unless you say yes."

"We're on opposing sides."

"Think how boring it would be otherwise."

Even her laughter held music. That voice alone could stir him.

"You intrigue me, Captain," she declared. "Why not?"

"The Melting Pot on Dearborn at say, seven-thirty? Will that give you enough time to take care of work?"

"Seven-thirty it is. See you later."

Chapter 7

Charlie maneuvered her car through clogged city streets. Happy she had shed her work uniform for comfortable slacks topped with a cashmere turtleneck sweater, she hoped she'd arrive at the restaurant at seven-thirty and not regret squandering time. She hated to be late for anything. Elated to find a space close to the restaurant, she parked at the curb. With an upward glance at the cloudless star-dotted sky, she didn't bother putting the convertible top back up and left the car.

Hurrying along the street, she checked her reflection in a darkened store window. Her stomach churned with another attack of nerves. Why had she accepted his invitation?

She hadn't dated since moving to Chicago. Her narrow focus on work left little time for a personal life and that had suited her. Her keen instincts on the job made up for her total lapse in judgment with Giovanni, and the brutal schedule served as a deserved penance. But it seemed Pat had her tossing caution aside.

The doorman directed her downstairs to the basement restaurant. Her eyes adjusted to the dim lighting as the host guided her to a secluded booth.

Pat rose as she approached; a dimpled smile brightened his face. *Lord, he's good looking.*

He waited until she settled in the booth before he slid into place across from her. The table quaked as his knee whacked its edge, shaking the water glasses.

"Ouch." She grimaced. "That must have hurt.

Are you all right?"

"I'm fine. Just one of the hazards of oversized legs and small tables."

"Do you want to change from a booth to a table? Would you be more comfortable?" Charlie surveyed the restaurant noting a few empty tables.

"No, I'm good here. I like the privacy." He squeezed her hand across the table and delicious warmth traveled up her arm. His face in shadows, his blue eyes gleamed devilishly.

Magnetic. His steady gaze held a suggestive undertow. Heat quickened deep inside her and a slow smile spread on her lips.

The waiter appeared to take their drink order. Reluctantly, Charlie slipped her hand out from under Pat's, away from that tantalizing connection to him, and accepted the menu the waiter offered.

"Good evening. Have you joined us before or is this your first visit?"

"I've never been here." Charlie arched her eyebrows as she glanced at Pat.

"I've been here a few times. If it's okay with you, I'll order for us?"

"Fine with me. I eat anything." She smiled and handed the menu back to the waiter. Pat conferred with the young man, placed their order and sat back in the vinyl-cushioned seat that creaked and crackled under his weight.

"So what's new? Get any wise guy scumbags off on technicalities today?" The passive expression on his face served to punch the smartass question harder.

The water glass froze on the way to her lips. "Screw up any more cases with shoddy police work today?" She sipped the water.

"Touché." A quick burst of deep bass laughter.

Very male. Very appealing.

"So..." She set the water glass down. "Do you

frequently invite coldhearted women out to dinner?"

He smiled and those boyish dimples creased his cheeks again. "I consider it a challenge."

Charlie's cheeks flamed. "You don't deny that you think I'm coldhearted?"

"Do you know your eyes darken almost to purple when you're mad? Hmm, very sexy."

Dangerous. Can't let my guard down for a minute. Disarmed, Charlie groped for a counterattack. "I would think you'd have enough challenges dealing with the Garbage Man Murderer."

Pat scowled and his narrowed eyes glinted steel blue. "It drives me crazy that the press comes up with a tag line for any criminal." Frown lines creased his forehead. He drummed his fingers against the hard wood table.

"We don't have anything," he continued, his expression grim. "And until we do, women die."

Regretting that she had dealt a low blow, Charlie touched the top of his hand lightly. "I'm sorry, Pat. I'm sure you're doing everything you can."

The waiter brought a platter piled with cut vegetables and hunks of bread and placed it in the middle of the table. Charlie relaxed, enjoying the waiter's culinary demonstration as he expertly mixed shredded cheeses with a generous amount of wine in a small black pot and then set it to melt on a burner at table center. The buttery aroma of the fondue wafted from the bubbling pot.

"Oh my. That smells amazing." Charlie's mouth watered. *Am I hungry for food or for that delectable man watching me silently?*

The waiter poured them each a glass of white wine, nestled the bottle in a bucket of ice and stood back. "Enjoy. If you need anything else just let me know."

Pat grabbed a skewer and pierced a hunk of

bread onto its tip, dipped it for a few seconds into the cheese mixture and rolling stray drips into the pot, held it, bread first, out to Charlie.

Instead of holding the skewer, she opened her mouth and let him feed her, enfolding her lips around the bread and sliding it off the skewer.

She chewed slowly, the velvety cheese coating her tongue. He focused intently on her mouth and frank desire reflected in his eyes.

Flattered, but rattled by the seductive appeal of his steady gaze, she commented lightly, "Mmm, wonderful food."

Suddenly very hungry, she picked up the skewer next to her plate, speared a hunk of cauliflower and dipped it in the pot. In a matter of minutes, she devoured more than half the vegetables and bread on the platter. Sated, she delicately dabbed her lips with her napkin and grinned. "Sorry. I missed lunch today."

Pat nodded a couple times as if impressed. "Don't be sorry. I'm used to eating with my brothers. You have to be quick or you go hungry. You put them to shame. I can't wait to pit you against them." He laughed. "My money's on you."

Charlie bit the corner of her lip. Did he really want her to meet his brothers? She resolved to curb her...appetite for Pat Sullivan and slow this down.

The waiter was back and Pat laughed as her eyes widened at the mounds of beef, shrimp, chicken and lobster morsels that he carried to their table on a platter. Barbarian hordes came to mind.

"There's more? I thought that was dinner." She pointed to the now obvious first-course platter where a lone piece of broccoli remained. "I would have paced myself."

"Would you like me to take this back, sir?" the waiter offered.

"No way." Charlie declared before Pat could

answer. "I can make room." She already had her skewer poised over a fat chunk of lobster.

Pat's hearty laugh boomed.

She and Pat polished off the next course rapidly, moaning with pleasure over delicious morsels and engaging frequently in bouts of infectious laughter.

"Dessert?" The hovering waiter was back, once again clearing plates practically wiped clean.

"No. No. No." Charlie held her hand up. The button on her slacks dug into her waist as she sat back against the booth.

"Dessert around here is cake, fruit, you name it—covered in delicious chocolate. Sure you want to miss it?" Patrick inquired.

"Don't try to tempt me. I couldn't eat another bite."

"Coffee or tea, miss?"

Charlie responded to the waiter's question with a simple groan.

"Just the check, please." Pat handed his credit card over to the man.

After he signed the receipt the waiter brought him, Pat slid out of the booth, sparing his knees this time. He donned his leather jacket and extended his hand to help Charlie scoot out of her seat.

His arm rested casually around her shoulder as they climbed the stairs and then occupied the same compartment of the revolving door. A masculine, citrus scent permeated the small space with his oven-like nearness. Wrapped in his enveloping warmth, Charlie walked the dizzy half circle out to the street, letting him steer her.

Outside, Charlie took a deep breath. The faint smell of chocolate filled the air. "Am I crazy or do you smell chocolate, too?" She tilted her head and looked up at him.

"Crazy, maybe," he grinned down at her. "But not about the chocolate smell. It's Blommer."

"What in the world is Blommer?"

"The chocolate factory. It's over on West Kinzie. My place is a few blocks away. Some Saturday mornings I wake up craving chocolate pudding."

Charlie stood facing him inhaling intoxicating chocolate pudding aromas, almost as heady as his clean, masculine scent. The force field of Pat's magnetic aura threatened to yank her smack against his chest and she experienced an urge to fly into his arms. Since she seriously doubted her taste in men, she couldn't decide whether to give in to the urge or resist and fly away instead. The silence grew uncomfortable.

If I leave now maybe I can workout an hour on the treadmill before they close the gym at my building. Burn some of this food and sexual attraction out of my system.

Pat checked his watch, a huge-faced timepiece on a black leather band that still looked puny around his wrist. "It's still pretty early. Want to walk off a little of the food?"

"You read my mind. I was just considering an hour on the treadmill at the gym in my complex." *To burn off calories and substitute as a cold shower.*

"Walking outside in the fresh air is so much better than a treadmill. Come on. Let's go look at the ships."

What's wrong with a little healthy attraction anyway? Charlie linked a hand over his downright thrilling bicep and he steered her around the corner, down the street toward Navy Pier. The Ferris wheel loomed ahead, a shimmering beacon in the dark.

****

Content holding Charlie's hand, Patrick strolled down the street totally enjoying himself. So far he'd describe the evening with Charlie as a success.

In companionable silence, he walked lazily with her beneath the mammoth Navy Pier iron sign. The tangy smell of the lake brought a wide smile to his face.

"This is my favorite place in Chicago. The water, the smell of cinnamon roasted nuts and the boats lined against the pier. There's no place like it."

"I don't know about that," Charlie disagreed. "Have you ever been to the Jersey shore?"

"No, I haven't. Occasionally a connection in Newark airport, that's about it."

"I think my boardwalk at the Jersey shore can give your pier a run for its money."

"Your boardwalk?"

"I'm a Jersey girl born and raised. My boardwalk has it all, the ocean, games of chance, rides and the smells of sausages, peppers and onions. I miss it."

"An East Coast snob." He laughed at her knit brows and combative expression. "My sister-in-law is from New York and that's what my brother, Joe, calls her. She usually punches him in the arm. Why did you leave?"

Releasing her hand, he slid his arm around her waist instead as they advanced toward the end of the pier.

"Long story." Her brows furrowed deeper and pain registered in her upturned eyes, a dark purple haze. She leaned against the iron railing at the end of the pier. The moon reflected on the calm waters of Lake Michigan.

Although curious about the long story that obviously carried pain for her, Patrick didn't question her. Charlie shivered. He slipped his jacket off and draped it around her shoulders. Brown leather swallowed her up to mid-knee.

"Thank you," she said softly.

A luxury liner docked slowly at the pier after a dinner cruise, churning a frothy wake.

"My family used to rent a house for a month

every summer somewhere over there." Patrick pointed across the lake toward Indiana. He laughed. "What a crazy time we had those summers. Dad had to work so he could only come on days off. We were on our best behavior when he was around, but the minute his car pulled away, we went crazy. Mom always controlled us, though. I'll never forget the last week we spent at that house."

Huffing another laugh at the memory, he continued, "My oldest brother, Danny, couldn't understand why our youngest brother, Jimmy, couldn't swim. Jimmy was three at the time, which made Danny about ten or eleven. The rest of us could all swim, something that came to us easy as breathing. Anyway, one afternoon he picked Jimmy up and threw him in the deep end of the pool." His hearty laughter boomed.

Charlie shoved a hand against his arm. "That's not funny."

"I guess you had to be there. Kay, who was all full of herself that summer after passing her junior lifeguard class, dove in the pool and hauled Jimmy off the bottom."

"What were you doing while all this was happening?"

"Not much. I was only five and I just yelled for Mom. She came running, grabbed hold of Jimmy, who was more shocked than hurt, and hoisted him into her arms like she'd never let him go again. My mother packed us all up one-handed and drove us home. We never went back to that house again. Hopefully we'll return again soon."

"What do you mean?"

"The house is for sale. It's pretty run down. My brothers and I have put in a bid. We want to fix it up and then the whole family can use it summers."

"You talk a lot about your family."

"I love them and they're a huge part of my life,"

he responded.

Smiling sweetly, her eyes softened. "It must be great to have such a big family."

"Few things are better. Except maybe this..." With a gentle flex of his arm, Patrick turned Charlie towards him. The wind freed tendrils of hair from her ponytail.

Impulsively, he slid the elastic band down the ponytail, and cupping his hand under the back of her hand, deposited it in her palm, as she stood silently watching him. Her thick, black hair tumbled down over her shoulders and blew free in the wind.

He threaded his fingers through the soft hair at the sides of her heart-shaped face. "I have wanted to get my hands on you all night," he said, his voice husky.

Patrick focused on her violet eyes. The color deepened to a smoky purple. He kissed her lips lightly, braced for her to resist. Maybe a slap in the face or a shove in the chest. But he was defenseless against the fiery sensual assault when she sank into the kiss, steeping him in the scent of gardenias, the faint taste of wine.

Her tongue flicked seductively against his lips. His breath came in gulps. He disengaged, uncertain he could maintain control in such a public place. His jacket slipped off her shoulders and fell to the ground as she reached up and held his face in her cool hands. Standing on tiptoes, she pressed sweet, soft lips firm against his. Patrick barely withstood the assault of his senses, his skin's surface chilled by the breeze while underneath his blood scorched through his veins.

A ship's horn blared in close range. Charlie jumped away, eyes wide, her hair a riot of midnight curls in the wind. She stooped and picked up the jacket, averting her eyes. His heartbeat slowly steadying, Patrick helped her wrap the coat over her shoulders again and then grasped her hand with a light squeeze. She didn't resist or say a word as she turned toward the pier entrance and they backtracked in silence.

He didn't regret kissing her and would relish a replay in the middle of the crowded intersection while they waited for a crossing light to turn. But he had detected sadness in her eyes for a second back at the pier and he reined in his impulse, unsure if he had somehow caused the emotion with his kiss.

Charlie stopped in front of a cherry red Corvette convertible parked a block away from the restaurant.

"This is mine." She flipped her thumb in the car's direction. "Thank you for a great evening," she stated, her tone stiff and formal.

"Holy shit. Are you kidding me? This is your ride?"

Delighted, Patrick circled the car, his fingertips trailing along the sleek lines and glossy finish. "This is every man's wet dream of a car."

Embarrassed, his cheeks heated. "I'm sorry. Not the best choice of words, but, well, holy shit, Charlie."

"Nicely put, Pat." She laughed. "It's just a car."

"Just a car. Are you kidding? This is a 1966 'Vette. The last year before they changed the model."

"Well to me, it's just a company car." She opened the door and slid behind the wheel. "Gets me from point A to point B."

The engine roared to life as she turned the key. *Sweet.*

"Goodnight, Pat." She pulled out of the space and hit the gas. Her musical laughter accompanied the throaty reverb of the 'Vette's engine.

Patrick stood in the middle of the street oblivious to the honking horns around him. *Damn, what a woman.*

He spent a split second peering at her head while he looped the tag over her foot. Good. No sign of the smug expression she wore earlier when he had handed over the bill in exchange for her underpants. He had effectively squeezed any smugness out of her.

Everything about her sickened him, as well as the sound of his next actions. Finished with her, he plunged a gloved hand down the neck of her shirt, fished the bill from her cleavage and pocketed it.

Paid in full. But not the way you expected, huh, bitch?

Dashing around the idling car, he slid into the seat. In neutral, he rolled the car toward the mouth of the narrow alley. No way to mute the growling engine but the ironic blare of sirens some distance away drowned out the car's rumbles nicely. Furtively, he checked each side of the sidewalk as the car breached the entrance to the street.

Ramming the gearshift into first gear and then a quick downshift into second, he roared away in the clear.

Chapter 8

Patrick debated leaving one of the two florist boxes in his car. He had volunteered to pick up the corsage of one white and five red roses for Ma from all her kids. At the florist shop, he had spontaneously requested another four red roses wristlet for Kay, remembering Mike's custom every year.

Mike would want her to have it. Leaning over the passenger seat, he scooped both up and swung the car door closed. Ambling through the parking lot, he rounded the corner of the beige brick building and stood in front of the church scanning the cars parked at the curb. Apparently, the first family member to arrive at Mother's Day services at the church, he leaned a shoulder against cool brick to wait outside.

"Mornin' to you, sir." One of two street guys squinted up at him from his perch on the church steps.

Stacking the plastic corsage boxes in one hand, Patrick plunged his other hand in his pocket and dropped all his loose change in the man's palm. Off duty, he wouldn't banish the man for panhandling.

"God bless you, sir."

His dad's Chevy Suburban rounded the corner and approached the church. Cradling the corsage boxes in the crook of his arm, Patrick stepped toward the curb and opened the passenger door for his mother.

"Happy Mother's Day, Ma."

Accepting the flowers and Patrick's kiss on her cheek with a smile, Jean Sullivan swung her legs around and leaned on his arm to exit the truck. The rear door swung open, discharging Kay's brood: Mikey with his long, muscled legs, Mary in a too short skirt and too high heels, the twins in matching party dresses and Mary Jane shoes, and his petite, too thin sister.

Her huge blue eyes glistened as he extended the corsage box toward her. "Happy Mother's Day, sis," Patrick greeted Kay, his voice soft.

Kay held the box in a limp hand and veered into Patrick's arms. "I'm trying, but I don't think I can ever be happy again," she whispered against his chest.

Brushing a hand over the crown of her head lightly, he smiled into her upturned dark blue eyes. When the tiniest smile twitched on her lips, he ruffled her short, spiky hair and grinned. "Sure you will, super mom. Your kids will always bring a smile to that pretty face. Let me." He eyed the florist box and opened his hand toward it.

She handed it to him. After he slipped the corsage on her wrist, he tossed the container in a trash can and offered her his arm. His mother herded the noisy kids up the steep stairs as Brian's jeep and Danny's Hummer pulled up in front. Car doors slammed as Sullivan women and children fell in behind Patrick and Kay entering the church.

Settling in what could only be described as the Sullivan family section in the rear, Patrick enjoyed the spectacle of the constant movement of his nieces' and nephew's little arms and legs. He made funny faces at Emma perched over Bobbie's shoulder in the pew in front of him, the baby's two-toothed, drooling grin his reward.

From the loft high behind him, sounded the choir's four-part harmony with heart-swelling beauty. The singers' voices silenced and the organ replayed the song's refrain. A chorus of shushes from the adult members of his family circus echoed.

From behind, a door swished open and then closed. A tall, shapely woman clutching an oversized book traveled briskly down the center aisle toward the altar, a blur of color. She wore a ruby red silk tunic over a short dark purple skirt and matching tights. A lacy purple cap like a fancy hair net contained her jet-black hair beyond a fringe of bangs. When she turned at the podium and rested the open book on the lectern, she cast familiar violet eyes at the audience. Charlie's coincidental appearance on the altar during his first time visit to this church astounded him. In her crazy colors, the woman was a human kaleidoscope. Just when he thought he had a handle on her personality, the kaleidoscope turned and he faced an entirely different, tantalizing creature.

Her face angelic, her lips neared the microphone, "Welcome to Assumption Church. Please stand and observe a moment of silence as we prepare to celebrate the liturgy today."

Patrick rose trancelike staring at her, an angel who had rebelled against the white dress code of heaven.

"Our gathering hymn can be found in the red songbook. Number 720, *Gentle Woman*. That's number 720."

Patrick dipped a hand toward the hymnal holder on the back of the pew and lifted the songbook, still riveted on Charlie. Pages rustled as the organ played a few bars. The choir accompanied her in song, as did the congregation, but still that velvety voice stood out, this time with honeyed sweetness in contrast to the driving sensuality of her stage performance.

He sang with gusto, his decent tenor voice perfectly pitched, while the altar servers, lectors and the priest processed down the center aisle.

"We begin this Mass in the name of the Father and of the Son and of the Holy Spirit," boomed the amplified voice of the priest.

When the congregation sat after the opening prayers, Charlie lifted her songbook and toting it in the crook of her arm, left the altar with a light trod up the left side aisle near Patrick's position in the pew. Confident that he stood out in the crowd of smaller statures he beamed at her. With a passive, blank expression on her face, she glanced at him, unsmiling.

Stung and confused that she had ignored him, he stewed. A blood-boiling kiss at the end of a windy pier repeated in his memory and he couldn't understand her frosty reaction to him now. She had to be bound for the choir loft but he'd be damned if he'd crane his neck and try to snag her attention up there after the rebuff.

With no mention of a second date after dinner the other night, he had no expectations to see her again. She didn't owe him a thing and vice versa. *Then why the hell do I care?*

The organ piped the opening bars of "Ave Maria" at the commencement of communion. Patrick sat back off the kneeler observing the forward rows of people snaking out of and back into pews when her haunting voice filled the chapel again. Curious when a duet sounded, her rich voice seemingly a harmony in stereo, he craned his neck anyway and glanced up at the choir loft.

I'll be damned. Twins? The multi-colored version of C. J. Demarco stood shoulder to shoulder with her mirror image clad in a white choir robe. The pair sang like opera stars, eyes closed. The sweet music stole his breath and tempted him to close his eyes, too, in reverent meditation. But then he'd close off the angelic sight of Charlie and, obviously, her sister of the earlier snub. He'd rather feast his eyes *and* his ears.

Kay's soft nudge on his elbow prompted him to stand and shuffle in turn toward the altar to receive communion. The music continued, and rounding the edge of the first pew into the center aisle, he peered straight up at the duo as he progressed to the back of the church, but didn't catch either's attention.

Determined to connect with Charlie after Mass, Patrick bent close to Kay's ear and whispered, "I'll meet you out in front of the church."

He slipped out of the pew as soon as the priest descended the first step off the altar.

Barreling through the vestibule and down the exterior steps, he took up position on the sidewalk and waited. Footsteps thudded and muffled conversations increased in volume as people streamed through all three doors and filed down the stairs on the heels of the priest. Patrick remained in place near the curb as the Demarco sisters descended the stairs.

"Pat?" Charlie stepped down the last two stairs ahead of her sister and strode toward him. "Are you stalking me?"

"Nice thing to say to a cop," he quipped.

Her brazen smile widened. "That doesn't answer my question."

"Lady..." He closed the distance between them to inches. "If I were stalking you, you'd never see me."

Before she could retaliate and despite the growing cluster of Sullivans in proximity to him, he kissed her. The slight forward pressure from her soft lips registered as pure pleasure. *Too bad I have an audience.*

He ended the kiss and her sparkling, lovely eyes held his.

"*Well.* Who might this kissing bandit be?" Red-and-purple clad sister confronted Patrick with disconcerting "Charlie's eyes" and an amused twist of her lips.

"Um," Charlie stammered. "Pat Sullivan, this is my sister, Emily. Emi, Pat."

"Pleasure to meet you." Patrick held Emily's outstretched hand and pecked her cheek with one eye on Charlie.

Brian and Matty strolled over, both wearing shit-eating grins and wide-eyed inquisitive expressions. Brian faced Emily. "Holy shit! You're the Bride of Frankenstein."

"Brian Michael you're less than a foot away from church!" came Mom's opinion of Brian's exclamation.

"Sorry, Ma."

"She used your middle name. You're in trouble, bro," Joe asserted directly in Brian's ear.

Emily chuckled, extending her hand toward Brian. "I take it you've seen the Graveyard Revue."

"Several times. Wow." That opinion earned Brian a playful cuff on the shoulder from his fiancée, Matty.

Emily shook Joe's hand next. "I'm Emily Demarco, nice to meet you."

Patrick swept an arm around Charlie's back and drew her forward toward Emily and the family. "Everyone, this is Emily Demarco, aka Bride of Frankenstein, and Charlie Demarco, otherwise known as C. J. Demarco, Esquire. Emily and Charlie, this is Joe, Bobbie, Emma, Danny, Molly, Amy, Deedee, Bree, Joey, Brian, Matty, Kay, Mikey, Mary and my parents Jean and John. There won't be a test." Smiles and nods as Patrick made the introductions.

"You've already met my nieces, Charlie. Emily, this is Peggy and this is Amanda, The Graveyard Rock N Roll Revue's biggest fans."

Peggy and Amanda's faces glowed with hero worship while shaking the adult twins' hands.

"Did you like the show?" Emily asked.

"Oh, we just *love* it!" they proclaimed in chorus.

Joe's head tilted toward Patrick's. "I knew C. J. was a woman, but *man.*"

"Yeah, by the way, thanks a lot. I really appreciated being blindsided in court."

A wicked gleam in his eye, he hovered near Patrick's ear and mumbled, "You holding out on me? You're cozy with C. J. Demarco?"

Patrick retorted, "None of your business."

Straightening his neck, Joe's snide expression transformed, addressing the women, the friendly, earnest host. "Room for more at your condo, Molly and Dan?"

"Always," Molly replied.

Joe didn't skip a beat. "Ladies, please join us for brunch?"

Squeezing Charlie's shoulder, Pat searched her eyes and confirmed Joe's invitation, "I'd like it if you'd come."

"I..." Charlie stared at Emily, apparently willing her to decline.

Patrick noticed her sister's mischievous expression and subtle nod instead of a headshake in reply to Charlie's unspoken question. "We'd love to," Emily said.

"Yes, thank you," Charlie muttered.

Her acceptance sounded like a concession, but he relished the idea to include her in a family gathering too much to care. *My family has excellent bullshit detectors.*

"Okay." Molly's clasped hands and drill-sergeant's tone a preamble to Sullivan family marching orders. "Pat, can you drive Charlie and Emily, please? Dad, you bring Kay and the kids. Brian and Matty why don't you leave the Jeep in the lot and ride with Joe and Bobbie. I'll clear everybody at the desk. See you in a few minutes." Molly herded her husband and kids toward the lot.

"Um...I..." Kay wrung her hands. "Daddy, could you possibly take us home? I think I'd rather spend the day with the kids there. Would that be okay?"

Dad's brow creased. "Sure, sure, sweetheart. We could do that, couldn't we, Jean?"

"Of course," Ma answered.

Brian held out his keys in Kay's son, Mikey's direction. "You can take your mom and sisters home in my car if you like, Mikey."

Mikey nodded accepting the car keys. "Uncle Bri?"

Brian shot Mikey a quizzical smile. "Yeah?"

"Would it be okay if you call me Mike from now on?"

Brian's lips tightened and he looked at his feet for a second. "Sure, Mike. I'll mention it to the others."

"Appreciate it." Mike crooked an arm, offered it to his mother and led his siblings to the parking lot.

"We'll head over to Danny and Molly's condo. Anyone want to ride with us?" Dad asked.

"No, we're good, Pop," Patrick responded, sending his parents toward their car.

The phone vibrated on his belt. He plucked it off and peered at the screen. Frowning, he declared, "Shit. I have to go."

"Patrick Michael you're less than a foot away from the church," Joe wisecracked. "Good thing Ma's out of earshot. Come on, Charlie and Emily, ride with us."

"Great idea," Patrick added. "I shouldn't be long."

"Pat?" Charlie edged closer to him. "Are you *sure* you want to leave me alone with your family?" she asked, implying who knew what she'd do behind his back.

"They can hold their own," Patrick stated. "Most

of them carry guns."

Charlie laughed as Emily linked her arm through hers. "Sounds like a blast. See you later, kissing bandit," Emily said in a breezy tone.

****

Patrick had never hurried official duties before and he wouldn't start now, but he was sorely tempted. Glancing at his watch, it might already be too late. The morning and nearly the whole afternoon had passed since he had corralled Charlie into Sullivan territory. She had probably already made a hasty exit from the get-together.

Patiently he managed to focus his full attention on Tom Gable's oral report scanning the ME's written report as directed.

"Is the sixth victim a hooker, too?" Patrick handed the report back to Tom.

"Uh huh. Same MO, identical scene, different alley." Shaking his head, Tom slumped in his seat. "I've got two guys from Vice consulting full time on it. How's the heat from the higher ups?"

"Somewhere between inferno and eternal hellfire. Jobs are on the line, Lieutenant."

"Yours or mine?"

He acknowledged Tom's stare with steely calm. "Do your job, Tom. I'll worry about the higher ups."

"I hear you, Cap. Okay if I round up some of these guys for canvassing?" Tom flicked his eyes toward the bullpen.

"Sure. Need me to pitch in?"

"Nah." Tom stood. "I've got it covered, sir."

****

Patrick sped toward Molly and Danny's condo. Had he left Charlie with the family to see if she could fit into his life? If yes, did he want that? *One thing's sure. I want her.*

Convinced she had already left, he hurried out of the parking garage anyway. Through the lobby,

up forty-three floors he exited the elevator.
Laughter, piano music and boisterous song filtered
through the cracked door.

Patrick flattened a palm against the door and
opened it. From the doorway, the interior space had
a fishbowl quality with a circular bank of floor to
ceiling windows and an open floor plan. *What the...?*
The family occupied every seat and some sat on the
carpeted floor. Their faces glowed rosy orange from
the sunset reflecting through the windows facing
west. Dead ahead with the looming Willis Tower as a
backdrop, his father and the Demarco twins grouped
around a baby grand piano belting out love song
lyrics. *"After tonight will you still love me? After I
have given my heart."*

Strolling into the living room, he returned
smiles as one or the other relative noticed him.
Charlie lifted her head off his father's shoulder and
gave him a crooked grin before picking up the
melody again. Emily, the piano player, gave a head
bob toward his father. "Take it, John."

John Sullivan's bell-toned tenor voice, which
Patrick figured he had inherited, filled the room.
"Will you still love me...like I...love...yuuuuuu?"

Applause. Whistles.

"Beautiful!" Charlie exclaimed whipping her
arms around his dad and hugging him with
uninhibited energy.

Emily rose clapping, her thighs pressed against
the keyboard's edge. "Bravo!"

Patrick stood thunderstruck, surrounded by
laughter and the remnants of the party he now
firmly regretted missing. Especially when Charlie,
smiling radiantly, let his father loose and
approached him with a tipsy gait. "Hey there, Pat.
I'm so glad you invited us."

*Sounds like she's "sho glad" I "invited ush." The
lady had enjoyed a few too many mimosas.*

Heading straight for him, she bumped into his chest, nestled her head there and laced her arms behind his neck. Looking back over her shoulder, "Didn't we all have the *best* time?"

His dad nodded and declared, "Yes."

"Sure did," Joe proclaimed.

Mom asserted, "Absolutely."

Charlie snuggled her head on his shoulder again.

Emily grinned at him, apparently delighted. "It was a blast." She beamed a smile at his father. "Thanks for singing with us, John."

"My pleasure." *Is Dad blushing?*

"I've got to run," Emily declared. "An evening performance at the park. Thanks everyone. Nice to meet you."

Pleasantries from the family followed Emily's progress toward Patrick. She tapped Charlie's shoulder. "Ready to leave, sweetie? I'll share a cab with you and you can drop me at the train station."

"I'll drive her home," Patrick volunteered.

Emily contemplated him, her arresting violet eyes penetrating as if she sized him up. "That's perfect." She pecked his cheek. "See ya, Pat. Take good care of my sister."

Chapter 9

Charlie eased into the car's oven-like interior and sat gingerly on the passenger seat that had obviously pre-baked on the top tier of the parking garage. The black leather seat radiated heat that glued her skirt to the back of her legs. Eyes closed she breathed deeply in the sauna as Pat turned the key and set the air conditioner to full blast.

The new car smell competed with his woodsy, lime scent. He maneuvered the car down winding exit ramps out to the street and steered with one hand through light, city traffic, casually holding her hand on the console with his right hand. Air from the vents blew wisps of hair around her face. The cool breeze against her brow lessened the dull headache that had already banished the mimosa high. The screechy instrumental music on the radio didn't help, though.

She leaned forward and jabbed her finger on the channel buttons, rejecting stations repeatedly, staccato blasts of sound.

Pat's brow furrowed. "What? You don't like jazz?"

"That shrieking actually hurts." Charlie cupped her ears with her hands.

"Oh, come on." He twisted his lips. "Kenny G was wailing."

Jabbing the radio buttons again, Charlie opined, "More like a cat wailing if you yanked its tail off. This is more like it."

Pat chuckled and hummed the pop tune she had selected.

Charlie sang, "*If there is any place on earth I belong, it's with you.*"

When he joined in, his tenor voice blended perfectly with hers. Her heart leaped, as it always did making pretty music, singing soulful lyrics. Their harmony during the chorus raised goose bumps on her arms. Her eyes closed, his warm, calloused hand enveloped hers again. Clasping it, she sang the last phrase with him at the top of her range, "*Make me, make me, make me fall in love again.*"

In the ensuing silence, the emotional power of their duet lingered. She wanted her hand back to break the hot current that seemed to flow between them, yet overpowering desire from his mere touch tempted her, too.

Opening her eyes, she stared out the windshield rather than risk a glance at him. The dizzying, titillating touch of his hand unnerved her as if he indeed held the power to "make" her fall in love again. The secret sentiments she had just expressed singing those lyrics cut too close to the bone. *He has me believing in falling in love again?*

She lowered her eyes to the floorboard, steadied her thoughts. *I can't forget just how far I fell, and more importantly, how I dragged my family over the cliff with me.*

Keep things light. "You knew all the words." Charlie pointed to the radio. "Don't tell me you're a fan of *America's Pop Star?*"

"Are you kidding? I voted ten times for Sage Thomas. He is the dreamiest."

Facing him, she burst out laughing at his guileless, wide-eyed expression. He turned his attention to driving, a dimple creasing his cheek in profile. She studied him, grinning, "Dreamy, huh? Something you want to tell me, Captain?"

Pat laughed. "Yep. The twins have me wrapped

around their pinkies. Every week we had a date to watch *America's Pop Star* together." He pitched his voice higher to mimic the little girls, "' Oh, Uncle Pat, isn't Sage just the dreamiest? You have to vote for him. Please, please.' How could I refuse?" he concluded in his normal deep register.

Charlie squeezed his hand, relishing the sensual tug the connection evoked. "You are a nice man, Captain Sullivan." Her body swayed toward him involuntarily.

Shifting squarely in the seat, she turned her head, gazed through the side window. *Maybe too nice to be true. I could fall hard for this guy. Who am I kidding? I want...*

The car entered the garage under Charlie's building. Pat braked at the curb.

Disappointment at the prospect of just "keeping it light" with him flustered her. "Would you like to come up?" She picked at the hem of her skirt. Afraid he'd say yes. More afraid he'd say no.

"I'd love to." He rammed the gearshift in drive, steered the car into a parking space with near whiplash results, unfurled that large body out of the car at breakneck speed and hurried around the rear bumper to open her door.

Quiet in the elevator, he scooped her keys off the floor after Charlie had dropped them the second time.

"Thank you." Her cheeks blazed.

"My pleasure." Handing the keys back to her, his expression pleasant, he exuded chivalrous patience while she fumbled with the lock like she had never opened a door before.

Nice, courteous Pat. But the smoky glimmers in his navy eyes belied the nice guy demeanor and hinted at the formidable aggressor beneath the calm exterior.

Charlie dumped the keys on a small table by the

door, turned and bumped into his chest. Gazing up into his eyes—sexy, smoldering—as hungry for her as she was for him.

Unbearably aroused, she stood on tiptoes, cupped his cheeks with her hands and pulled his face toward hers. Their lips met—hot, demanding, shifting in consuming motion. She linked her arms around his neck to anchor her quaking body. His powerful hands kneaded her rear and he lifted her off the floor, their mouths fused.

Charlie wrapped her legs around his waist, his erection pressing at the tender center between her legs. Biting need gnawed inside her. She wanted quick, hot, no-time-for-second-thoughts sex with this man—right now.

"The couch," she commanded, two quick bursts of language. And then she tasted his lips again, addicted to his breath-robbing response to her kisses.

Melded to him at the hips, Pat shuffled her over to the couch and gently released her down onto the cushions. He balanced over her, propped on his arms. Their eyes locked, his hazy blue, questioning.

Hands flat on his back she tugged him down on top of her in answer, flattening her breasts beneath the welcome, necessary weight of his body on hers. His hand wedged between their aligned thighs, his knuckles grazing her feverish skin and yanked her skirt up to her waist. His fingers edged under the leg of her panties, caressing her, stroking, sending shockwaves coursing through her. She shook her head back and forth on the couch pillow. "No, no, no. I want you inside me. Now, now, now..."

Thank God, he didn't argue as he twisted sideways and removed her panties one-handed.

He offered no resistance when she grasped the zipper on his pants. Tugging it open, she freed him, enfolded his velvety smoothness with her hand and guided him inside her. She moaned as he filled her. Her muscles tensed in gathering, racing need as she matched his thrusts while her heart pounded in her ears. Deeper and deeper his body fused with hers and still it wasn't enough.

Nothing mattered but the exquisite elevating sensations he incited, layer upon layer. Charlie dug her nails into his back as mounting passion seized her, stopped her breath. In the same split second, they reached a shattering climax. "Yes, yes, yes..." Charlie exclaimed.

"Charlie..." He collapsed on top of her. Her name on the pinnacle of his release brought a rush of pleasure. Then his arm muscles flexed and he rolled, half sitting, and leaned against the sofa back.

"Wow..." His voice was a throaty growl.

"Yes, wow." Her voice was a whisper. She should feel guilty. *I just slept with the police captain! But, oh my God.* Her body hummed and she had no regrets.

His eyes steady on hers, she detected vulnerability, warmth and frank affection in them. *Not coldhearted anymore?* She smiled. Rubbing her hand over his shirtfront, she caressed in wider circles on his chest, inching closer to his waist.

"Again?" His eyebrows lifted.

She answered with a suggestive smile that spurred him to his feet. He shed his pants, white briefs atop muscular legs and he scooped her into his arms and off the couch.

"The bedroom?" he asked.

She pointed a finger toward the closed door at the end of the hallway and giggled. Unaccustomed to surrendering control, she allowed herself the luxury to be literally carried away. She nestled her head against his hard chest. Shifting her to the cradle of one of his arms, he balanced her body against his hip and turned the door handle. The door swung open into her pitch-black room.

Readjusting her in his arms, he questioned. "Lights?"

"Just open the drapes. There'll be plenty of light. There's a home game tonight."

"What?"

"You'll see. Just pull the cord on the blackout drapes over there."

As he tugged on the cord, she slipped in his arms. Apparently possessing remarkable reflexes, he squatted and contained the freefall before she landed on the floor. When he stood with a rapid upward surge, the roller coaster effect jostled her in his arms. The rush exhilarating, she laughed. "What a ride."

Reaching out an arm, she grabbed the cord and opened the drapes. Bright light flooded the large room through floor-to-ceiling windows.

****

Patrick turned toward the windows squinting. "What a sight." He traveled the few feet to Charlie's bed, plopped her down and reversed back to the window.

"Hey! Thanks a lot," she sputtered.

He glanced over his shoulder. She lay on her side on the gray comforter, propped on an elbow, grinning.

Eyes drawn back to the spectacle below, he remarked, "That's Wrigley Field down there."

"Oh really? I never noticed. Thanks for pointing that out," she replied dryly.

He stooped and opened the vent window near the floor. A crowd cheered, a muted roar. Wrigley Field blazed below, a monumental neon pie. Glowing white baselines cut a diamond in the vivid green field, Cubbies at bat.

Awed at the aerial view, Patrick shook his head. "I can hear the announcers. And you can just stand here and watch home games. Amazing."

The sweet-spot crack of bat against ball and a tiny white dot sailed over the outfield bleachers.

Pumping an arm in the air, Patrick added to the fans' wild cheers yelling, "Home run!"

"You're striking out in the bedroom over here."

He turned around, beaming a smile at her, "Can't have that." But he couldn't resist another quick glance out the window. "I can even see the scoreboard."

"Let me guess. The Cubs are losing."

"Damn, they are. How did you know?"

"Because they always lose. They suck."

"They don't suck."

"Up against my Yankees they do."

"Oh God, a Yankee fan. I should have known. I'd put my Cubbies up against your Yankees anytime."

"Good luck with that. My Yankees would kill them."

Patrick turned toward her. She sat in the middle of the bed. Her hand slowly unbuttoned her blouse. His mind blanked, eyes riveted to the slow descent of her fingers. He cleared his throat and retorted, "Bull."

"Knick."

"Very funny. I get it. All of your New York teams are superior."

"I knew you were smart. Facts are facts." Her blouse flapped open now and he leveled his eyes on her. Her brazen, bratty expression challenged him. He took a step closer to the bed. His shins bumped against the footboard. *Two can play the same game.*

"Bears." He grabbed the front of his shirt with both hands and wrenched it open. Buttons sprayed everywhere clattering on the marble floor.

"Giants, or even the Jets." She tossed her shirt on the floor, his sailed on top of hers. Plucking at her bra straps, she slid them off her shoulders releasing full creamy breasts. Arms at her sides her nipples pebbled in the air-conditioned room.

His eyes widened. *What a sight. She is beautiful.* He yanked off his belt one-handed, heaved it atop the pile of clothes and knelt on the bed.

"Lou Malnati pizza. Deep-dish," he declared.

"Famous Ray's."

His hand reached towards her breast. "Willis Tower."

She snickered. "No contest. The Empire State Building."

His hand cupped her breast as his eyes glazed. She knelt in front of him.

Boldly, she stared into his eyes, daring him to make the next move.

Slowly, tenderly, he touched his lips to hers. He tasted oranges and champagne as he deepened the kiss and she returned it with increasing demand. He trailed a hand over one shoulder, down to caress the contour of her breast while he explored her mouth, a pulse-spiking duel of tongues.

He teased the skirt's zipper down by fractions of an inch until it slid into a pool around her bent knees.

He finally had her naked except for pale cream thigh-high stockings.

Heart thundering, he wrapped an arm around her back, satin skin electrifying his fingertips with sensation. Her deep purple eyes smoldered, spellbinding, offering no opposition as his face inched closer to hers. He nipped her lower lip lightly with his teeth, covered her mouth again with his. A sigh escaped her parted lips into his mouth, one breath. Cupping her breast in his hand, he kneaded its unbearable softness, his nerve endings sizzling.

Her eyes held his as she snagged the waistband of his briefs with two hands, stretched it wide, pulled them down around his knees and lay down on the bed, legs parted. Ready to take his time with this, he dotted kisses up the inside of her legs slowly. Her muscles clenched and relaxed beneath his lips in waves. He used his mouth and his fingers to torture her, his own arousal nearly killing him. She came on a gasping intake of breath, her head thrown back.

The black tousled hair, the puffy lips—her utter surrender drove him wild. Patrick balanced over her, his arms straining, muscles bulging. The tip of his erection pressed on the soft vee between her legs. Her eyes closed, she undulated her hips against him, to capture him, a torture that brought him to the edge of restraint. But he held back, teasing her and depriving himself to drive her as insane as she drove him.

She wrapped slender but surprisingly strong arms around his back and flattened him on top of her with a downward thrust. Lost in the scintillation of her softness beneath him, his will dissolved and the intention to take it slow disappeared.

Entering her enveloping heat, he frantically matched each powerful thrust of her hips. Thrashing her head back and forth on the pillow, she moaned. Then pleaded, "Now, now, now. Oh God. Please now!"

Unable to hold back any longer, he clasped the cheeks of her rear end and thrust deeper inside her, a more frantic rhythm now. The swell toward climax seemed to rise from the center of her, volcanic, towing him upward until she simultaneously cried out his name and he released, a shattering intensity that was almost blackout.

Even though his bones seemed to have dissolved, his arms trembled. His fingers dug deeper into the soft flesh of her bottom positioning her on top of him as he rolled on his back. In no hurry to lose this intimate connection with Charlie, Patrick held her tightly in his arms and gently stroked her silky hair, her shoulders and back.

Charlie nestled against his chest panting. Her lips tickled his chest hair, "Mind-blowing."

"Yes," he managed.

A second passed, a minute?

Raising her head of glorious, tangled hair a smile creased blushed cheeks. "Unbelievable."

Patrick grinned as she slid sideways and cuddled next to him, one stocking encased leg straddling his thigh.

The delicate lace band that circled her leg mid-thigh seemed a miracle of engineering. "How does it stay up like that?"

Charlie propped up on an elbow and narrowed her eyes. "Didn't you learn that in sex ed class?"

"Hmm." He pointed to her hose.

"Oh. There's elastic in the lace." She slid the band down to the bend of her knee and he intercepted her hand.

Rolling the silky material back up her thigh, he marveled. *Her skin could compete with the finest silk on earth.* "It's very sexy. I've never seen anything like it."

"You are kidding me."

"I've seen my share of stockings held up by garters but nothing like your magic stockings." Smiling, he slid his hand under the lace.

"I bet your sister wears them."

He blew a puff of air between his lips and withdrew his hand. "Well, thanks for that mental image."

Charlie laughed at his reaction and rested her head back down on the crushed pillow. "Okay, how about your sisters-in-law?"

"You're killing me." Patrick chuckled. "I never think sexy and my sisters in the same sentence."

"You are adorable." She kissed his cheek. "It was great meeting your family today. Your mom is so sweet. I bet she wears thigh-high stockings."

"Enough!" Hugging her close to his chest, Patrick closed his eyes, must have dozed.

When he awoke, he was covered with a sheet and she was curled next to him, watchful.

Smiling into her soft violet eyes, he murmured, "Sorry I fell asleep." He tightened his stomach muscles to sit up.

Her hand pressed on his chest and he lay still.

"Can you stay?" Her tone bashful, her wide eyes implored him, vulnerable. No trace of the imp or the vixen that had claimed his body.

"There is no place I would rather be." He kissed her, and pulled her closer.

****

The smell of coffee woke Patrick with a start. A pillow replaced Charlie by his side. He swung his legs, sat on the side of the bed and rubbed his face with his hands. Bright sunlight streamed through the glass door.

What time is it? He stared at his watch in disbelief. *Eight o'clock! When was the last time I slept so late?* Charlie had piled his neatly folded clothes on the chintz chair in the corner, one of her magic stockings on top. Eager to see her, Patrick tugged on his pants and strode into the living room. Wrapped in a white puffy robe, a towel wrapped around her head, she stood in front of panoramic windows facing the lake.

He circled her waist with his arms, drew her close and kissed her neck. "Good morning, angel."

"The kissing bandit strikes again."

Patrick jumped as if the statement had branded him. He stumbled backwards and crashed into the piano bench. Emily's contagious laughter filled the room and Patrick laughed, chagrined. "I thought you were Charlie."

"Happens all the time. Not often enough with

handsome men, though." She smiled and leaned against a metal window sash. "Charlie left over an hour ago. She said she left a note on your clothes. Did you miss it?"

"No, I got it." He grinned remembering the stocking. "I'll get dressed and out of your way." He turned around and headed toward Charlie's bedroom.

"Take your time. Charlie's shower is amazing. Give it a try."

When he had finished taking an invigorating shower, he dressed and left the bedroom. Emily sat at the piano picking at the keys.

"Have a great day," he called out as he paced toward the door.

"You, too. Hey, bandit!"

Patrick turned to face Emily, one hand on the doorknob.

The Demarco twins' haunting eyes pierced him. "Don't hurt my sister."

Chapter 10

The cab whizzed through the intersection bumping over a manhole cover.

"You can stop on this side across from Paddy's Pub," Charlie directed the driver.

After he complied, she handed him a ten-dollar bill and waited on the curb for traffic to clear.

Charlie had no qualms about ditching work early to dress for the early evening date—totally out of character. *Only eight hours at the desk on a Saturday when I should have put in ten. I should be out-producing everyone for that full partnership, should be focusing on the plan.*

Cars crisscrossed in front of her. *Late night conversations with Pat, staring at the empty pillow next to me and wishing him there instead of on the other end of the phone or bubbling with anticipation to see him today aren't in the plan, either. I don't care.*

A white stretch limo rolled to a halt in front of the pub on the other side of the street and a man emerged from the car towering over its hood. He faced her on the sidewalk, talk, dark and gorgeous, a kelly green patch over one eye. *Joe Sullivan.*

"Hi!" Charlie called, stopping on the divider line halfway across the street.

Joe grinned and responded, "Hi, Charlie." He offered a hand in turn to the women exiting the car.

Sprinting to dodge an oncoming car, Charlie joined the group: Bobbie, Matty, Molly, a woman she didn't recognize, then Brian, Danny and a bearded man with the body of a weight lifter.

"Where's Pat?" Matty inquired.

"Maybe inside? We agreed to meet here," Charlie answered.

Matty smiled and clasped Charlie's hand, towing her a few steps toward the unidentified couple. "Charlie, this is my brother, Shamus Connors and his lady, Cara O'Shea. This is Charlie Demarco, Pat's lady."

Pat's lady. Unbridled pleasure warmed Charlie's cheeks at the notion. "Nice to meet you." Charlie extended her hand in Shamus' direction. He grasped it and hauled her into a burly hug and then let her loose so Cara followed suit.

A medley of hugs for Charlie from other family members followed until Joe hollered, "Let's go."

Matty linked arms with Charlie and they all trouped inside behind Joe, a temporary plunge into near blindness contrasted with the bright, early evening sunshine outside. Only a few patrons sat at the expansive mahogany bar in the cozy pub that smelled of furniture polish and yeasty beer. Joe waved a hand to the bartender, a Pierce Brosnan look-alike who might be Paddy. Down a narrow hallway behind Joe, the partygoers progressed single file through an open door.

Charlie chuckled, glancing at the backs of the men's matching Irish green T-shirts that bore the screen print message, "ANOTHER SULLIVAN BITES THE DUST."

Pat faced the doorway as Charlie entered the private room. His identical "bites the dust" shirt the perfect color with his red-blonde hair. Electric blue eyes crinkled at the corners and cheeks dimpled with his disarming smile. Maybe twenty other people milled around or occupied living room style chairs and sofas grouped around cocktail tables. But only Pat seemed present to Charlie, walking toward her, everyone and everything else a blur. Her earlier bubbling anticipation overflowed and she rushed toward his approach, into an exuberant embrace.

Pat squeezed Charlie tight and flattened her breasts against his solid chest. A man you could lean on, trust to catch you if you fell. Safe, sheltered, valued. *Nothing in the world I should be doing rather than spending time with him.*

"Mm," Charlie sighed, raising her eyes to meet his. "It's so *good* to see you."

He pecked a soft kiss on her lips. "Same here." Dimples bloomed and he leaned down, whispered, "I'll kiss you like I want to later, okay?"

Charlie smiled, nodded. He circled his arm around her shoulder and steered her to a forefront seat to join the immediate family. Joe slid a mug of beer toward her across the coffee table, poured another and handed it up to Pat who propped a hip on the arm of Charlie's chair.

Molly passed Charlie a plate, heavy with a slice of shepherd's pie. "This stuff is to die for. And we're having chocolate bread pudding for dessert."

Charlie sampled a forkful of pie. "Delicious."

"Time for a toast," Pat declared as he stood, his booming voice silencing the sounds of conversation in the room. "To Brian and Matty's engagement and impending wedding. Neither of them wants a traditional bachelor or bachelorette party, so this is a triple-purpose celebration. The wedding date's set in October. When..."

He cast a wicked glance at his brothers who popped up on their feet on the cue, beer mugs in hand. In unison they chanted, a rap beat, "Another one bites the dust!"

"Sláinte!" Pat proclaimed.

"Sláinte!" came the partiers' chorus.

Charlie sipped her beer as Pat dragged a chair arm to arm with hers, sat and leaned close. "Come to the wedding with me?"

"I..." Charlie's breath caught in her throat. "That's almost four months away. I don't know what my schedule will be like. It takes gargantuan arranging just to rework things for an evening like this..."

"If you want something enough, you can always work things out," Pat asserted. His eyes full of conviction, his gaze held hers.

He's serious, wants a future for us. If Pat had treated their relationship casually, Charlie might have been able to behave the same way, too. No strings, live for now, two consenting adults, why not? No misplaced trust.

Charlie stared into his magnetic eyes and perceived only honesty in their sapphire depths. *What do I want?*

Her answer sprang from her heart. "I'd love to."

"Good. It's a date." Pat picked up a plate and dug a fork into the food.

Charlie ate, too, surveying the room. "Are these people friends of yours?"

"Yeah, through Brian and Joe. A couple of Brian's neighbors, one of Matty's. Mostly they're guys from the Arbor Village precinct in the western burbs. Co-workers."

"Ah. I'm seriously outnumbered. These are the folks who've given me the nickname, Shooter and Piercer, or something like that."

"Nah," Joe mumbled over a mouthful of food. He swallowed and then said, "It's Shot, Pierced and Your Collar's a Free Man. You know, after your law firm, Schotz, Pearson and Freemont."

Charlie snorted and cast Joe a condemning glance. "Perhaps you're the author of the nickname, Officer?"

Joe gave her a cocky, one-sided grin. "I take the fifth, Counselor."

Amid communal laughter, a three-ring binder

changed hands until Danny, seated to Charlie's right, set it in her lap. She fingered the edge of the notebook, "What's this?"

"Karaoke catalog," Danny replied.

"Oh, no." Charlie picked up the book and held it out in front her gingerly as if it contained explosives.

"You have to go first, Charlie, you're the only one here who can carry a tune," Matty asserted. "Besides, I haven't had enough beer yet to take a turn."

"Pat has a nice voice." Charlie extended the catalog toward him.

Brushing it away with a wave of one hand, Pat grinned at her. "Hey, you're the pro. Show everybody how it's done."

"Geez." Charlie plopped the binder in her lap, opened it and perused the song list grumbling, "Big difference pretending to be my sister, pretending to be a character than standing up and doing a solo here."

One song choice struck Charlie as a possibility. "Brian, what are some of the last names of your buddies here?"

Brian's eyes scanned the room. "Let's see. O'Brien, Daly, Nagle, Lynch, Johnson, Esposito...why?"

Close enough. If I'm the hated death of justice to these cops, at least I can play to the crowd. Charlie slid a song request slip out of the front pocket of the binder. "Thanks, Brian. I have a pick now." Pulling the pen out of the tab on the inside seam of the notebook, she used it to scribble a selection and passed the book back to Danny.

Molly and Danny hovered over it, pointing at various choices, laughing. Slips of paper piled up on the coffee table. Joe stood, notebook in hand, and scooped up the papers. Handing them to the DJ, he circulated the binder to another group.

"Charlie, you're up," boomed the DJ.

Utter silence in the room. Charlie rose and sashayed to the mic, stage fright expanding inside her like a balloon. The intro bars of piano music sounded, a key she could manage, and relief flooded her senses. Lyrics appeared on the huge plasma screen, but she didn't need them to belt out, "*When Irish eyes are smiling...*"

Cheers, glasses clinked together. She gathered confidence, even overlaid a soft lilting brogue. "*...you can hear the angels sing.*"

Locking on Pat's smiling eyes, she finished with a flourish. "*...sure they'll stee-eel your heart...away.*"

Piercing whistles and appreciative clapping. Loving the hearty acceptance despite her professional reputation with the majority of the guests, Charlie threaded her way back to relinquish the hot spot at the mic to somebody else.

Drinking beer and eating chocolate bread pudding, Charlie increasingly enjoyed the party and the performances. The Sullivan couples, sentimental and obviously crazy in love with each other, touched her heart. Didn't matter that the voices were hardly show quality.

Molly and Danny sang Faith Hill and Tim McGraw's "It's Your Love." Bobbie and Joe rocked with "Ain't Nothing Like The Real Thing." Glasses clinked after Matty and Brian finished a sweet rendition of "Tonight I Celebrate My Love For You."

"Aw," the DJ proclaimed. "What a pretty couple. Okay, up next..." He referred to the slip of paper, "Patrick."

The wide smile Charlie bestowed Pat extinguished when he grabbed her hand and tugged her to her feet. "Hey!" She laughed. "Once was enough."

"C'mon. This is a duet. Sing with me."

Submissive, Charlie let him lead her by the

hand to the mic. A quick glance at the lyrics displayed on the screen. Delighted, Charlie widened her eyes. Pat winked at her as he sang the first verse to "Islands In The Stream."

Answering him with the second verse, she placed her hands over his, palm to palm, and faced him. Bridging into the chorus together, her voice pitched easily to a Dolly Parton-like soprano and Pat sang the Kenny Rodgers alto.

Charlie's delight grew, enchanted with the sound of their voices' harmony.

She belted out the last refrain, warming to the import of the lyrics, how in sync they were in the duet—as a couple. At the end of the song, they brought down the house. Even the DJ gave them a standing ovation. Mentally "sailing away" with Pat, Charlie reeled.

Pat slung an arm around her waist on the trip back to the table. Wanting the party to go on a few more hours and wanting to be alone with him carried equal weight for Charlie. Pat tilted the balance in favor of leaving when he invited her to his home.

Outside in the mild evening, he commented, "My house is a few blocks from here. Want to walk or should I hail a cab?"

"I'd much rather walk."

Strolling with him, a possessive hand cupping his bicep, Charlie's happiness soared higher with each step. They rounded a corner onto a street lined with brick row houses, a deceiving vintage neighborhood atmosphere scuffing new construction sawdust underfoot. Pat led her to the stoop of one of the identical residences, turned a key in the lock and opened the door for her to enter ahead of him.

Charlie roamed inside. The foyer opened into a homey living room with mismatched, high quality furnishings: a dark green leather sectional, a multicolor footstool, marble-topped coffee table, a Scandinavian teak lounge. The same musky, lime scent as Pat's aftershave permeated the air. Blindfolded, she'd recognize this place as his.

Pat pocketed his house keys and slouched against a wall, watchful, a half smile on that beguiling mouth.

"I love your house. Eclectic," she remarked approaching him.

"When Kay redecorates it's first come first serve for the brothers to lay claim to rejects."

"I think your furniture is beautiful." Charlie beamed at him.

"You're beautiful." A couple feet away from her, Pat shoved away from the wall and opened his arms.

On a half fly, Charlie rushed into his embrace, on tiptoe sampling that luscious mouth, melting, spinning, hungrier to kiss him than any other man before. Hanging in his arms, their lips crushed together, teased apart, tongues clashed in dizzying, scorching passion.

She experienced a sensation similar to flying as he lifted her into his arms. "My bedroom's upstairs."

Charlie tucked her head into his shoulder, her lips pressed to the side of his neck. Already in motion, Pat mounted the steps in twos. Charlie's stomach fluttered in the rise and fall of the climb.

Pat switched on the upstairs hall light with his elbow and then swung her through the open door into a dark room. Not stopping to turn on the light, he headed straight to the bed, dropping her gently on the mattress. He stretched her arms overhead, held them down with one hand and covered her mouth with his. Urgent, demanding, consuming, he ravished her with searing lips.

Her arms pinned above her head, his hand explored freely down her neck, across her breasts, sliding under the band of her jeans, flat against her abdomen until his insistent fingers on the tender flesh between her legs immersed her in a burning state of pure desire, incessant need.

Eyes closed, her heartbeat pounding in her ears, she panted, "I want..."

His mouth covered hers again. *You.*

Freeing her hands, he unbuttoned her blouse, dragged her bra straps down to expose her breasts and trailed his tongue over her nipples. She ran her hands over his shoulders, the muscles in his broad back, grabbed fistfuls of his shirt and tugged. Sweeping the shirt up over his head, she tossed it on the floor while he undid her jeans and stripped them off, taking her panties with them. She lay on the bed, every nerve ending on fire, her breath ragged, while he stood to dispense with jeans and boxers. Naked, glorious, his powerful body arched over hers. Aching to make love with him, she opened her arms.

His body blanketed hers and, at last, he filled her, a mind-blazing, runaway ascent to a vast, sparkling place of piercing, exquisite release, *precisely* what she wanted. Trembling beneath him she circled his neck with her arms, clung to him, eyes closed in the divine aftermath.

"Am I too heavy for you?" Pat mumbled against her neck.

"No, stay. You're just right."

He lifted his head, his eyelids half closed, rumpled, adorable. "Stay with me tonight."

She pressed her lips against his, warm, gentle. "For now. I'll have to leave early."

He rolled, his strong arms cradling her. Her head on his chest, she drifted to sleep, her last waking thought an unspoken: *I love you.*

Hooded navy blue eyes focused on his reflection in the floor-to-ceiling mirror. The repetitions clicked off in his brain: two hundred and one, two hundred and two. Positioned on a padded, black, leather bench he leaned over and pumped the dumbbell up and down. Muscles flexed and trembled, veins bulged and yet he continued the cadence. No rest as he strived for perfection. Reaching two hundred and fifty reps, he switched hands and started the count again. No rest.

Looking good, my man, looking good. The ladies at the bar last night were impressed, writing their numbers on napkins, the whores. Sweat dripped slowly down his chiseled chin and landed on his naked chest. His hand slid under the waistband of his silky black shorts and moved concurrently with his other hand's movements, stroking. The release was short and unsatisfactory. The twenty-five pound weight thumped to the rubber mat barely missing his foot. He stalked to the weight rack and grabbed a heavier weight, pausing to run his hand seductively down the bat that leaned against the paneled wall. Yes, I know what the ladies want. Disgusted, he glared at himself in the mirror. They don't want me. He heaved the weight into the mirrored wall. Glass shards rained down on the floor. Damn them all. He stomped out of the room, the bat gripped in his fist. Time for batting practice. The gym door slammed behind him.

Chapter 11

Shirlee leaned against the brick wall. *I'm so tired. Just a little sleep. That's all I need, a little nap.* She yawned, closed her eyes and dozed. Her head drooped backward bumping on the wall and woke her roughly. Digging through the oversized bag that hung on her bony shoulder, she grabbed a pack of cigarettes and a lighter. Tapping the last cigarette out, she crumbled the pack, threw it in the gutter and flicked the lighter with her thumb. Inhaling a satisfying lungful of smoke, she paraded along the sidewalk, wobbly on bright red high heels.

The full moon cast a creepy glow on the deserted street. Not a car in sight. She squinted at the scratched face of her battered Timex. *Three o'clock already. Mrs. Jarvis will only hang in another hour with Lincoln. Then she'll leave him alone again. Damn it.* She needed a trick soon or would return home empty handed again after a night's work.

A quick flick of her fingers sent the red-tipped cigarette butt skidding a foot ahead of her aching feet on the walk. She stomped on it and then leaned against a bus stop sign, too exhausted to continue "advertising."

The metal dug into her back, another discomfort she was too deflated to do anything about. *Please God. You know I'm trying to change, trying to make a better life for my boy. A couple more months and I will have my diploma. I promise as soon as I can get a job, I'll stop. Please God, just help me now.*

The soft rumble of a well-tuned engine reverberated in the stillness as two narrow, beams speared the gloom ahead, the car's headlights like a jungle cat peering out of the bush. *I'm dreaming, right?*

A sleek neon orange sports car glided to a halt in front of the bus stop, a futuristic shuttle. The driver gave her the once over and then he smiled. The window near her glided down. "You working?"

"Might be for the right price, handsome." *Awesome freakin' car. Not bad looking. Look at those muscles. A real pretty boy. Nice and clean. I've done worse. Must be something wrong with him. Maybe a cop?*

"Name your price." His smile never reached his cold, dark eyes.

"Yeah, sugar. Then you drag my ass in and I'm locked up for the night. Cost me a bundle to get out. Good try. But I'm not biting, asshole." She shifted away from the signpost, stood facing the side of his car and considered ditching the shoes and bolting.

He barked a laugh. "You think I'm a cop?" His gloved hand waved a wad of bills over his head. He threw two bills out the passenger window. They fluttered and then landed on the curb.

Two hundred dollars! Sold! Since when do cops drive cars like that anyway? "All of a sudden I feel like working. What's your pleasure?" She bent from the waist slowly to give him a calculated display of her full breasts plumped up by her too-tight bra, snatched the bills and slid them seductively into her cleavage.

"Get in and we'll talk." She minced to the car, her feet burning in the stilettos and opened the door.

"Damn these cars are hard to get in ladylike." She lowered herself into the deep bucket seat, her legs spread awkwardly. Facing him, she wet her lips with a circular, suggestive sweep of her tongue.

"Ladylike?" He snorted. "You are something, aren't you?"

His disdainful tone stung. "I don't get any

complaints." *Asshole. Curb it, Shirlee. Don't blow it now. You got a live one.*

"Take off your panties and hand them over for a first installment." He held a hundred dollar bill just out of her reach.

"That's easy." Plunging her hand in her bag she pulled out a pair and then snatched the bill. "It's been a busy night, sugar," she lied.

He tossed the panties behind his seat, revved the engine and accelerated away from the curb. His hand brushed the grip of a bat propped between the seats, its bulk hard against the left side of her leg.

"What's with the bat? Are you a ballplayer or something? You look familiar. Are you famous?"

"Not yet, but I'm working on it. I'll be very famous one day." He chuckled.

Dollar signs danced in Shirlee's mind. She sat back and relaxed, thanking God for her new meal ticket.

A few minutes later the car swerved into a long, dark alley lined with Dumpsters. The moonlight cast horror movie shadows against the buildings lining the narrow passage. A chill crept up Shirlee's spine.

"This is where you live, Mr. Important?" All bravado, she opened the car door as soon as the car stopped and squeezed out, disgusted that she had been so gullible. At least she still had his three hundred dollars. All her instincts screamed, *Run!*

Her right ankle buckled painfully against the asphalt in the damned heels and she staggered forward, windmilling her arms.

"Hey!" He overtook her in an instant and towered over her. "This is just a shortcut to my place. Come on." His gloved hand dug into the soft skin of her underarm. The muscle of his arm bulged against the tight, black, silk T-shirt.

She shoved on his hand with no effect. "Let go! You're hurting me."

His grip tightened as he jerked her along behind him, deeper into the alley.

"I'm not going anywhere with you." She tried to plant her feet, but the stilettos skidded along the pavement as he effortlessly yanked her behind him. *What did you get yourself into now? Think!*

"Help! Help!" she screamed.

The punch snapped her head back. Pain exploded in her head as her cheekbone surely shattered, a crunching, splintering sound. The salty tang of blood filled her mouth. Dazed and dizzy, she slumped downward, her vision dimming, darkening. Her knees hit the ground, more splintering sounds as the gravel scraped off skin.

Stay awake, Shirlee! What about Lincoln? Adrenaline surged through her body at the thought of her son. Twisting with a hard jerk to the left, she landed on her side, kicked both her legs out. One shoe flew off her foot and sailed into the Dumpster; the other foot connected painfully with a rusty, bent shopping cart, toppling it over.

Helpless on the ground, she couldn't escape his grasping hands around her neck, a vise, squeezing. She clawed at his leather gloves trying to dislodge the strong fingers. Blood dripped from her lips and tears stung, blurring his nightmare face, twisted with hatred.

"Don't," she grunted, a choked whisper. *Why me? What did I ever do to you?* Her lungs on fire, begging for air, Shirlee envisioned her son's smiling face and knew she'd die without answers. *Oh my poor baby. Lincoln, Mommy loves you. I am so sorry, baby.*

"Leave my stuff alone!" a man yelled, the shout an echoing miracle.

The chokehold released abruptly and Shirlee gasped, sputtered, blessed air ripping down her throat like acid. Her mind reeling, she swiveled her head toward the unknown savior's voice. He stood by the Dumpster, swinging a plank of wood.

Rolling, bleeding stripes along the pavement, Shirlee squeezed under a Dumpster. She jumped as something connected with the metal, sending shockwaves through her, an ear-splitting racket. Panting, she observed naked toes poking out of an ancient pair of sneakers held together with duct tape at her eye level. A long coat dragged on the ground. Her knight in shining armor banged his piece of wood again on the Dumpster, a metallic din.

"Leave my stuff alone! Get out of here!" he bellowed. Long, gray, matted hair draped on his shoulders and over a wild, ZZ-Top beard. She didn't know what smelled more, the garbage or her hero. She had never seen anything more beautiful in her life.

The avenger chased her attacker back to his fancy car and threw the piece of wood in the air as the car roared backwards out of the alley.

"Thank you," Shirlee mumbled, so indistinctly he might not have heard. The small effort to speak hurt her throat unbearably. Clutching her neck, she lay limp on the ground.

Mumbling unintelligibly, the man righted the dented cart, stuffed the bags that had fallen next to the Dumpster back into the metal basket and then pushed his way deeper into the alley.

Shirlee painfully inched out from under the Dumpster and attempted to stand. Dizzy, she sank to her battered knees. *I have to get out of here. What if he comes back? Please God, don't let him come back.*

Gripping an edge of the Dumpster, she heaved upright. She took one tentative step and her legs buckled. Collapsing, she hit her head hard against the Dumpster as she fell.

****

Patrick awoke with a start at the jarring sound

of the alarm. Hugging the down pillow against his chest, he gazed at the empty mattress next to him, disappointed. Charlie was gone, although her luscious gardenia scent permeated the sheets. He tossed the pillow on the floor and stretched his arm out to jab the snooze button on the clock. The buzzing continued. Naked he jumped out of bed and retrieved his cell phone from the pants he had tossed on the floor last night.

"Sullivan," he barked into the phone in motion toward the bathroom.

"Sorry to wake you, Captain. I think we finally got our break."

"No problem, Gable. Tell me." Patrick punched the speaker button and propped the phone on the soap dish in the shower, opening the faucet full throttle. Beneath the pounding hot spray, a hint of Charlie's delicate fragrance blossomed in the steam. He smiled at the thought of her naked in his shower.

"We've got a live victim. Garbage Man Murderer's MO. Attempted strangulation of a streetwalker. A white female was brought into Chicago Regional about a half hour ago. Semi-conscious, markings around her neck."

Patrick turned off the jets, stepped out of the shower stall and wrapped an oversized black terry towel around his waist.

"According to the admitting doc's report, her cheekbone is shattered and her windpipe's bruised," Gable continued. "She's pretty beat up. One big black shiner with the eye swollen closed and her cheek puffed out like a balloon. Punched, I'd say by a pretty heavy hand. Major bruising and welts around the neck."

Reaching into the stall, he plucked the phone off the tray and switched off the speaker. Holding the phone to his ear, he leaned against a towel bar. "Did you question her?"

K. M. Daughters

"Spent a couple minutes with her before I called you."

"What did she give you?"

"Nothing. She's closed up and refused to speak with me. She's putting up a fight against being admitted, too," Gable replied.

Straightening, Patrick slipped a hand towel off the bar, scrubbed it over his wet hair. "So, how's this a break, Tom?"

"Well, sir, a security guard found the victim lying unconscious next to a Dumpster in an alley. One of the nurses told me that when they brought her in, she was mumbling something about a baseball bat."

His pulse accelerated, a familiar burst of awareness that an investigation was gelling. "Keep her there. Stand guard at her room until I arrive. Call Frank and get him over there, too. No one gets in. Understand? I don't want any leaks on this. I'm on my way."

"Understood, sir." Gable clicked off.

Patrick's heart pumped with adrenaline. *Finally, a break in the case.*

The brightness from the overhead light glowed off the snow-white tiles. Patrick squinted at his face in the mirror above the sink. His hearty laughter echoed at the sight of a lipstick kiss on the mirror reflecting smack dab in the middle of his cheek.

She must have climbed up on the sink to position it just right. You are a minx, Counselor. Her playful calling card brought a rush of longing. *More laughter, more kisses, more Charlie.* Nothing compared to that perfect moment when nothing existed but her.

No woman had ever invaded his senses like she had, with such apparent ease. *I love her.* The knowledge seeped into his consciousness bringing a spontaneous burst of elation.

He brushed his teeth, rinsed the brush and replaced it in the cabinet staring at the outline of her lips, grinning. His smile widened as he ran a comb through his hair.

The woman had him spinning. All business, up the ranks ambitious Patrick was weak-kneed with happiness the "morning after."

Chapter 12

Patrick stood, barely fitting into the tight space at the foot of the victim's bed. The privacy curtain bowed outward, draped in the shape of his back. As reported, the woman was battered, her left eye swollen hideously in a blackish knot. Below the eye, her cheek was a black-and-blue balloon. Inflamed welts and bruises circled her neck. She regarded him with one eye, woozy, her eyelid fluttering frequently.

"I'm Captain Sullivan, Ms. Davis. Are you feeling well enough to answer some questions?"

"No, no, Lincoln..." The bed covers pitched with her agitation. She clutched the corner of the sheet. "Gotta go home." Straining to sit, she slumped flat again, apparently exhausted from the effort.

"It's okay, ma'am." He moved to the side of the bed, clasped her feverish hand in his. "My detective is on his way to your home. He'll bring your son here."

Her free hand covered her heart and she heaved a sigh. "Thank you." She eyed him warily, the hand in his, shaking.

Patrick touched the top of her hand with his other hand to reassure her and then swung an arm sideways to pull a chair bedside. He sat, still linked to her hand. "Can you tell me what happened?"

The terror registered in her brown eye, skittered tremors through their connected hands. Patrick's size either intimidated or soothed—the inquisitor or protector. In this case, he hoped the latter.

"Fancy car..." Her breathing labored, she blinked her eye rapidly. "I was working..." She tugged her hand out of his grasp, her eye cast downward.

Interpreting her hesitation, he said, "There'll be no solicitation charge, Ms. Davis. You can tell me the truth."

She nodded. "Name's Shirlee." Nodding repetitively, she took several labored breaths. On an exhalation, she mumbled, "Baseball freak...bat..."

All his senses quickened and his mind raced to formulate the questions to probe her memory, find the investigative thread. "He hit you with a bat?"

Shaking her head, "In car...orange..."

"The bat was orange?"

More head shaking.

"He drove an orange car," Patrick surmised.

Shirlee nodded assent, her head drooped on the downturn.

"Stay with me, Shirlee." Stroking the top of her hand, Patrick waited. In a soft voice he continued, "Let me see if I understand. The john picked you up in an orange car. You saw a baseball bat in the car. He drove you to the alley where a security guard found you this morning. What happened when he stopped the car in the alley?"

She swallowed with effort, flicked her tongue on her bottom lip, grimacing.

Patrick studied her face. "Would you like some water?" Without waiting for a response, he rose, filled a plastic cup from the pitcher, slid the paper wrapping off a straw and plopped it in the cup.

Seated again he bent the head of the straw, held it to her lips. She swallowed a sip and emitted a mewling sound, squinting her eye in pain.

Patrick placed the cup on the bedside table and then clasped her hand again. "Take your time, Shirlee. He brought you to the alley and then what happened?"

"Punched in the face," she said. "Fell down. I

kicked...choked me." Her breath came in little puffs. "Bum..."

"Bum?" His mind raced. "Someone else was there?" *Saints be praised, a witness.*

Shirlee nodded. "Stopped...grocery cart..."

A tear beaded in the corner of her eye. "So scared. Blacked out..."

Patrick's stomach dove, disappointed, deriving more questions than answers in her recounting. Who was the witness? How could they find him? *At least an orange car could be a differentiator.*

Shirlee's breathing steadied as Patrick absently stroked her hand again. "That's all," she asserted, her voice clearer, stronger.

"We have to catch this guy, Shirlee. When you're well, will you agree to work with a sketch artist? Get his description out there on the street?"

Closing her eye, she nodded agreement, gave him a weak smile.

He stood smiling back at her. "Good. That's good, Shirlee. I'll let you get some rest." Releasing her hand gently he patted it and took a business card out of his jacket pocket. He displayed the card to her and said, "I'll leave my card on the table here." He laid the card down. "It has all my numbers. Call me any time if you remember *anything* more."

"Sure."

His back to her about to part the curtain to leave, a finger snap sounded. Patrick turned to face her.

"Home run," she declared.

Confused, he probed, "Something he said?"

"No." Shirlee grinned, a lopsided proposition with her misshapen, swollen face. "The plates on the car."

Two broad strides and Patrick was at her bedside again. "Thanks, Shirlee." He beamed at her.

"Any time." Shirlee's head bobbed up a down, her lips a determined line. "Catch that son of a bitch and lock him away."

Speeding toward his office, Patrick stole a personal moment to leave a message on Charlie's voice mail. "Dinner tonight, Counselor? I'd like to return that kiss you left me. With interest. Can't wait to see you."

Satisfied, he disconnected the phone, pulse racing, triumphant. *This amazing woman in my life and a concrete bead on the garbage man asshole.*

****

Phones bleated, conversations rumbled, his men moved around the rectangular space at work, a beehive of activity. Striding down the aisle in between the rows of desks at the stationhouse, he inquired, "Anybody see Gable come in yet?"

Nobody had, so he stopped at Lucas' desk, would give him a shot at exoneration for the search warrant fiasco. "Good morning, Josh. Run some plates for me?"

"Sure, Cap. Whatcha got?"

"Vanity plates spelling home run," Patrick said.

Propping a hand on the edge of the desk, he leaned over the sergeant's shoulder peering at the monitor. Lucas hunted and pecked on the computer keyboard, brought up the Illinois Secretary of State vehicle registration portal.

Patrick gave him a light tap on the shoulder. "I'm going to get a mug of coffee. Want some?"

"No thanks, sir. I'm good."

"Be right back."

Bristling with anticipation, Patrick marched to the coffee machine, filled a mug and returned to Lucas' desk to check on his progress.

Eyes wide, Lucas flicked his head toward the computer monitor, "Take a look, Captain."

Patrick set his coffee mug down on Lucas' desk.

Leaning over, nose close to the computer monitor, he read the data line. "Registrant JACKSON MORGAN, III, 23 W. Shadybrook Lane, Lake Forest."

On an expelled breath, Patrick concluded, "Fuck."

"The senator's kid." Lucas leaned back in his chair and cast a questioning look up at Patrick. "What do you have on him?"

"That will stick?" He combed his fingers through his hair. "I'll request an arrest warrant for battery and attempted murder. A search warrant, too, for his car and residence."

Wagging his head, Patrick continued, "We probably won't find anything incriminating at the residence, but it's worth a shot—maybe something that ties the victim to the car, but it's doubtful. I hope to God that while we have him behind bars on lesser charges, we can build the rest of the case."

"Who'd he beat up?"

"A hooker named Shirlee Davis. Tried to strangle her in an alley lined with Dumpsters. Ring a bell?" Patrick arched his eyebrows.

"Sounds like the Garbage Man Murderer's MO," Lucas commented, scratching the side of his face.

"I'd stake my reputation that Jackson Morgan III *is* the Garbage Man Murderer, Josh."

"Damn." Lucas stared at the monitor again. "You're gonna need oven mitts to handle this potato."

Patrick snorted. "You're probably right."

Picking up his coffee mug, he inquired, "Want in on the arrest?"

Lucas' face lit with a broad smile. "Hell, yeah."

"I'll nail down the warrants with the DA and speak to Gable when he gets in. You can roll with him to pick up the senator's scumbag son."

"Thanks, Cap. I appreciate it."

Patrick started down the aisle toward his office, hesitated and backtracked to Lucas' desk. "Josh, not a whisper about this to anyone. That's an order."

"Yes, sir."

"Ask Gable to come see me when he gets in."

"Sure."

****

An hour later, Patrick glanced up from his paperwork at the sound of a deep voice. "You wanted to see me, Captain?"

Tom Gable paused outside his open office door, proceeded to enter at Patrick's nod and sat in the chair in front of the desk.

"I have a warrant for the arrest of Jackson Morgan III for the assault on Shirlee Davis." He handed Tom the paperwork.

"Is this *the* Jackson Morgan? The politician?"

Patrick stood, restless. "His son."

"Sir, I'm positive the perp with Shirlee Davis is the serial killer."

He gazed steadily into Gable's eyes. "Me, too. So, go arrest the guy on these charges and help me find the evidence to connect him to the murders."

Gable pinched his lips together. "I'll give you everything I have on this, sir."

"I know you will, Tom. Take Lucas with you on the arrest. Morgan will lawyer up in a New York minute," Patrick said. The cliché reference to New York shot Charlie into the forefront of his mind. *My East Coast snob.*

"I'm very good at reciting Miranda. Anything else, sir?"

"When we get Morgan processed, I want Captain Flynn Dowd brought in on a consult. We'll see if he thinks this guy fits the killer's profile."

"Yes, sir."

"And I want round the clock protection for Shirlee Davis and her son. I'll work with the prosecutor to make sure we handle her with kid gloves. Tomorrow at the latest, I'll talk with her again, show her Morgan's mug shot. She told me that a bum in the alley drove him away, saved her life. I'll want a sketch to put out an APB." Patrick pursed his lips. "Snowball's chance we'll ever find this guy, but I can dream."

"You think we can sweat a confession out of Morgan for the murders?" Gable narrowed eyes.

"Hell no," he huffed. "But we'll buy some time with the battery and attempted murder charges to bring him down on the murders."

"I'm with you, sir." Gable unfolded from his seat and swung out the office door.

Chapter 13

Charlie inhaled and counted to five before she pressed the intercom button to stop its annoying buzz. She hadn't taken time to eat or even use the rest room for hours, buried in unfinished preparation for an appearance in court the next day.

"Carrie, please, I said no interruptions." She released the button, shifted in her king-sized leather desk chair and continued to read the brief in her hand. The buzzer blared again and interrupted her hard won concentration.

Doesn't anybody take Sundays off around here? "Carrie what *is* it?" Frustration evident in her strident tone.

"I'm sorry to interrupt C. J., but Senator Morgan's office is on the line. The senator is demanding to speak to you," came Carrie's rushed explanation.

Charlie let the brief drop on her desk. "Me? Why me? The senator is Mr. Freemont's client."

"Mr. Freemont directed the call to you." The plaintive tone in her assistant's voice made Charlie feel guilty for the earlier abrupt dismissal.

Knitting her brows, Charlie probed, "Did he mention what this is in reference to?" *I've never worked on any of the senator's files.*

"No, he didn't," Carrie replied curtly.

"Okay, Carrie. Sorry for biting your head off. Give me a few seconds, then put the call through." Charlie added the brief to the stack of papers on her desk, opened the oak drawer and placed a fresh legal pad on her pristine blotter. Her mind raced. *What does he want with me?*

The firm's entire staff coddled, pampered and practically worshipped the notorious senator. Yale alumni and roommates, Jamie's father and Jackson Morgan, Jr., now a popular senator, created the "good ole boy" network in Illinois. When Freemont, Sr. retired last year, Jamie inherited the senator and his assorted legal problems. Charlie suspected dubious ethics were involved when the senator played Jamie's puppeteer, a frequent occurrence, but she hadn't been directly exposed. A half million-dollar retainer demanded service, and Charlie hoped she was up to the presumed command performance. Her stomach clenched when her phone rang.

Inhaling and then exhaling slowly, she answered, "Senator?"

"Please hold for Senator Morgan," a nasal voice, and then elevator-style Muzak filled Charlie's ears. She tapped the pencil on the pad in time with the tune, hoping she'd dispense with this quickly so she could return to digesting the brief, put something in her rumbling stomach, return Pat's call, have a life...

"Little lady, how are you today?" The senator bellowed, a blast against her eardrum.

Charlie frowned and held the phone a few inches away from her head. She wouldn't even think about his reference to her as "little lady." That would only lead to her voicing her opinion of sexist, demeaning word choices—surely followed by a boot out the venerable doors of Shotz, Pearson and Freemont without a salary.

She modulated her voice, "I'm just fine, sir. Thank you for asking. How may I help you?"

"Well, honey, I have a little problem and I told Jamie only the little lady in your firm can handle this."

"What is the problem?" *"Little lady." "Honey." There's no use saying anything to this man.*

"The police arrested my boy. They just waltzed into his home, waving papers under his nose, started rummaging through his things, put him in handcuffs and led him out. Stuffed him in a squad car in broad daylight. Thank God, the newspapers didn't get wind of it. Do they have any idea who they are dealing with? Heads are going to roll."

Hopefully, excluding my head. "When did this happen? Do you know specifics about the papers you mentioned? What are the charges?" She scribbled her personal brand of shorthand on the pad, starting case notes, the scratches indecipherable to anyone else.

"Damned if I know. He called me on his cell phone the minute he answered his door and was told he was under arrest. They made him hang up but they did say they intended to take him to the downtown station, not the local one in Lake Forest. I'm furious. My driver's taking me to the First District station on State."

Pat's office. Pleasure shimmered through her at the memory of singing with him, strolling hand in hand, those massive hands skimming her body.

Senator Morgan broke through her reverie. "...in my car on the way to the police station. I expect you to meet me there and get my boy out now."

The call clicked off in her ear before Charlie could respond, protest—conduct any sort of a two-way conversation with the senator. Accustomed to his minions jumping to serve him, she apparently was expected to be his minion, too. Her mind whirled. Retainer or not, she wouldn't do the man's bidding blind to the facts.

Charlie stalked down the corridor to Jamie Freemont's corner office. His door cracked open, she shoved through it and encountered her boss seated behind his desk, phone to his ear, running his hand through his disheveled hair. The sun dipped low over Lake Michigan, an orange halo behind him. He waved her to one of the barrel chairs in front of the expansive, uncluttered glass-and-chrome desk.

"Thanks, Frank, I owe you." He hung up the phone, whistling through his teeth and stared straight into her eyes. Head wagging he said, "We've got trouble, C. J."

She opened the spiral notebook and waited, pen poised over the meager file notes from the senator's call. No need to ask which case Jamie classified as "trouble."

"My guy at the police station filled me in."

"What's the evidence?"

"The victim is a prostitute. She claims a john attacked her and attempted to strangle her to death and would have if a vagrant hadn't wandered into the alley and interrupted the crime. She identified his car, his license plate and confirmed his identity as Jackson Morgan, III, from the mug shot just a few minutes ago. She's in the hospital, apparently badly beaten."

"Her word against his so far. Fingerprints? DNA? Do they have the vagrant?" Charlie rattled off.

"No."

"Does the senator's son have a record?"

"He's clean. No prior arrests, not even a traffic ticket," Jamie responded.

"So what's the problem? A hooker versus an upstanding, rich citizen. Which judge in this town wants to get on the senator's bad side? Cut-and-dried. I'll have him home in time for the first pitch of the Sox game." She snapped her notebook closed and started to stand but plopped back down in the seat when Jamie's face set in a grave mask.

Her empty stomach knotted in dread. "What aren't you telling me?"

"This info stays in this office."

"That goes without saying," she assured him,

her heartbeat escalating.

"The police suspect that Morgan is the Garbage Man Murderer."

"Oh, come on." She searched Jamie's serious eyes for a hint of humor, couldn't find it. "How is that possible?"

"They have evidence that has not been released from the other cases that implicates Jackson Morgan III in those serial murders."

"What evidence?" She tapped a drumbeat on the notebook with the pen.

"My guy got closed mouth. Won't tell me."

"Damn it. This changes everything. I hate being blindsided." She checked the slim watch on her wrist. "I have to go and meet with the senator and his son. Call me if you can find out anything."

"Will do. Good luck. Get that boy released."

"Luck won't have anything to do with it." She rose and paced towards the door. Midway, she turned around and faced her boss. "You know this family, right?"

Jamie nodded.

"Give me your honest assessment," Charlie insisted. "Could the senator's son be a serial killer?"

Jamie shook his head. "Absolutely not. He's a well-raised, privileged all-American type. A politician is ruthless in many ways, but the senator is a good man, a great statesman with spotless family values."

Appeased, Charlie returned to her office and sat at her desk. An hour later, she still sat there, reluctant to follow the inevitable course involved in this case. The Tiffany lamp cast a rainbow of colors across the paper in front of her. She slipped the paper into a folder, squeezed it into her bulging briefcase and slipped her pumps back on her swollen feet. Resigned to do battle, she switched off the light.

****

Charlie peered through the smoky window of the attorney consultation room at the police station. Senator Morgan leaned his long, powerful frame against the pale green wall. The sleeves of his tailored, crisp white shirt rolled to the elbows, he exuded his trademark man of the people persona. A younger muscular man lounged in an orange plastic chair, an air of inconvenience on his otherwise blank face.

Pat is somewhere in this building. Her head dipped with heartache and piercing regret. After a deep, cleansing breath, Charlie opened the door and entered the room. The senator's face bloomed with an expectant smile as he pushed off the wall to face her.

When his son remained slumped in the chair, the senator slapped him on the back of the head. "Stand when a lady walks into a room, boy. Where are your manners?"

With obvious, deliberate slowness, the younger Morgan rose from the chair to his approximate six-foot height and extended a meaty, manicured hand. "Hey."

"Hello." Charlie tried not to wince as he shook her hand, his bone-crushing delivery inconsistent with the innocent smile plastered on his face. "Please sit down, gentlemen."

Charlie took a seat at the small table.

"Yes, *ma'am,*" the son responded, contempt ringing in the statement as his butt hit the plastic seat with a crack.

The senator scraped a chair along the floor, positioning the back at the edge of the table and straddled it, facing Charlie. "I want my boy out of this jail immediately."

"I can't promise anything." She checked the clock on the wall behind the senator. "It's late. It's Sunday. The bail hearing won't be until tomorrow morning."

"Unacceptable. My son did nothing wrong. I want him out now." He flipped out his BlackBerry as he stood and moved to the corner of the room, spoke in a hushed voice, each muffled syllable punctuated with his fist in the air.

Charlie addressed the senator's son. "Mr. Morgan."

"My friends call me Jack."

Ignoring the come-on, half smile, Charlie continued, "Mr. Morgan, do you understand the charges against you?" Before he could reply, Charlie read from the paperwork the police had provided. "Battery. Attempted murder."

"This is a case of mistaken identity. Honestly, do I look like the type of man who could hit a woman?" He turned on the full wattage, white-toothed smile. Dimples creased his tan cheeks.

The dazzling smile never reached his strange, emotionless, blue-black eyes. There was something off about the grin that she couldn't put her finger on.

Tamping down a surge of repulsion, Charlie continued questioning him in even tones. "Where were you between midnight and five o'clock this morning?"

"A gentleman never tells." He smirked and winked.

"A gentleman facing jail time does." She stared willfully into his inky eyes, gratified when he trailed his gaze away first.

"Were you at Karen's again last night?" the senator asked without raising his eyes from his BlackBerry's screen, apparently texting.

Jackson the third squinted at his father. "Yes. I was with Karen last night. I'm sure she will vouch for me."

Perplexed, Charlie eyed her client strongly suspecting dishonesty. "I'll need Karen's name and phone number."

"No problem." The senator placed his business card on the table in front of her. "Karen White is an intern in my office. Just call my office and they will put you through to her."

Charlie's cell phone buzzed in the pocket of her briefcase. Normally, she would let the call go to voicemail but after a quick glance at the screen, she took the call. "What's up, Carrie?"

"Mr. Freemont has Judge Stone's agreement to hear the bail request for Senator Morgan's son tonight."

Amazed, Charlie could only respond, "Really?" She jotted in her notebook. "This came directly from Mr. Freemont?"

"Sure did, C. J., Courtroom 42 as fast as you can get there."

"Thanks, Carrie." Charlie snapped the phone shut and slowly returned it to the briefcase pocket.

"Judge Stone will hear your bail request tonight. They are waiting in Courtroom 42. I'll speak with the guard to arrange to transport you, Mr. Morgan." She glanced at the senator, noted that he wasn't the least surprised with this unusual scenario. "Senator, would you like to accompany me?"

"Allow my driver to take you there, little lady."

****

The senator remained glued to his BlackBerry and ignored her. During the brief car ride and seated outside the courtroom waiting for the accused to arrive, Charlie focused on the statement she would make before the judge until the bailiff called her and the senator into the room.

The prosecutor, clad in a rumpled, ill-fitting corduroy blazer over wrinkled jeans, a dazed expression on his face, stood behind a wooden table on the right side of the room facing the judge's bench. Charlie walked forward, shook his hand and then took her place next to Morgan III at the defense table. In the hushed room, the esteemed senator took the end seat in the first row behind her.

Her opponent referred to a sheet of paper in his right hand and cleared his throat. "Judge, in light of the charges of battery and attempted murder the State requests that the defendant, Jackson Morgan III, be held without bail pending trial. Thank you." He plunked down on the wood chair, which made a squeaking sound as it scraped across the floor.

Charlie's mind raced. *No mention of any other charges. Maybe Jamie was wrong about the connection to the murders.*

Relieved and exhilarated, she stood and smiled at the judge. "Good evening, Judge. Thank you for hearing this bail request in such a timely manner. Jackson Morgan III is an innocent man. He can account for his whereabouts"—Charlie paused, the words temporarily stuck in her throat—"for the time of the assault."

"The defense requests that the defendant be released on a personal recognizance bond. There is no reason for Senator Morgan to supply bail money. His son will plead not guilty and is not a flight risk. Mr. Morgan's good name means everything to him and he is eager to stand trial where he will prove his innocence. Thank you."

The judge declared, "Request for release granted. I see no reason to require a bond in this case, if I have your assurances that you will not leave the state and will appear for trial against these charges." He cast a questioning glance at the defendant.

"You have my word, Your Honor," Morgan III asserted, an earnest declaration that sent unwelcome chills through Charlie.

Obviously satisfied with the outcome, the senator pumped Charlie's hand. "Good job,

Counselor."

"I want to speak with Karen White in the morning," she reminded him, distaste for her role in this matter nauseating her.

"I will make sure she's available for your questions."

"Thank you. Good night." Charlie plucked her briefcase off the table and left the courtroom, the hollow clicks of her heels on the wood floor matching the hollow sensation in her gut.

Jamie Freemont stood in the hallway. "Out on bail?"

"Even better. No bail was required."

"Thanks, C. J. I can always count on you to do flawless work." Jamie smiled and moved to put his arm around her shoulder.

She sidestepped away from the arc of his arm. "Really? Then why do I feel like I need a shower?"

Charlie tramped down the hall. The senator's voice echoed in the hallway as he congratulated Jamie on the quick bail hearing.

This is just wrong. I know he's guilty. What if he's guilty of more than just assault? She felt dirty and used. *This is what my life has come to?*

Charlie reached down and extracted her cell phone from her briefcase, turned it on and shoved through the heavy courthouse doors with one free hand. The chilly wind bathed and refreshed her face. Her brisk pace was just what she needed to clear her mind. She stopped, sat on a bus stop bench and listened to Pat's message again.

"Thank you for the kiss on the mirror." His burst of laughter brought tears to her eyes. "But I would much rather have one in person. How about tonight? Call me." *There won't be a kiss tonight or any night. When Pat finds out I'm defending Morgan, he'll want nothing to do with me.*

Her finger shook as she hit call back. Thankful

for his voice mail, she left her message as tears flowed unheeded down her cheeks. She resumed walking home, deciding to send the letter she had drafted earlier via messenger in the morning. The memorized words haunted her.

Dear Pat, I have decided to take a case that poses a professional conflict of interest between us. For the duration, it's imperative that we stop seeing each other privately. Please understand. Love, Charlie

****

Patrick had his phone to his ear when Sergeant Lucas stomped into his office and tossed a piece of paper on his desk.

Skimming the paper, he blurted, "Son of a bitch. He's out already."

"Judge Stone released him fifteen minutes ago. How the hell did that happen so fast?" Lucas paced in front of the desk. "Laws don't apply to the freakin' politicians who make them."

After listening to Charlie's message, Patrick knew exactly how Jackson Morgan III had been released. "My bet is he got himself the best lawyer money can buy."

Patrick swept the anger and hurt into the back of his mind, but unanswered questions plagued him as he tried in vain to reconcile this attorney with no conscience and the sweet woman he loved. *How can she defend men who abuse and murder women? Worse, how can she free a serial murderer? Maybe she doesn't know whom she's defending. Shit, what if she does?* Maybe he didn't know C. J. Demarco at all. Maybe he didn't want to.

Chapter 14

Shirlee sagged onto the sofa with a huff the minute she closed the door behind Lincoln. The simple tasks to make him a peanut butter sandwich for lunch, stuff it in his school bag and kiss him out the door had consumed her meager store of early morning energy. The scabs on her knees, elbows and hands pinched and itched, tempting her to prod them with her long, fake nails. Her face in the mirror that morning had downright frightened her, a distorted, multi-colored bruise ringed with her brown hair hanging in greasy strings.

Every inch of her body ached, except for her swollen face where unrelenting pain throbbed and rang in her ears. The ringing increased and expanded. Covering her ears defensively, the sound muted and she realized the telephone caused half the clanging. Weary, she reached for the portable and glanced at the caller ID. *Private.*

Intending to take her frustration out on the assumed telemarketer, she answered, "Take me off your list," her voice gruff and two registers lower as if she had smoked two packs of cigarettes the night before.

"Madam, I'd like nothing better," came a silky male voice.

"Beg your pardon?" The words snagged in her sore throat and she coughed, instantly regretting it. Massaging her neck gently she managed, "Who is this?"

"I'd like to speak with Mrs. Shirlee Davis, please."

He sounded nice, polite, but there was a false ring to his courtesy that made her distrustful. "This is Miz Davis. You didn't answer my question. Who are you?"

"I'm Senator Morgan..." he paused.

The name was vaguely familiar but her head was muddled with pain medication and she wasn't in the mood for games. "I don't have any money for campaign contributions. Goodbye."

About to click the phone off, his voice boomed, "Wait!"

"What do you want?" she screeched back into the phone, all patience gone.

"You have accused my son of attacking you and I want to convince you that you're mistaken."

Her eyes narrowed as the mental fog cleared. "You're that bastard's father? And you're a s*enator*? That's rich. No, sir. I'm not mistaken as you say. *Goodbye.*"

"If you know what's good for you, you little whore, you'll listen to every word I have to say," he hissed.

"What the hell..." She sputtered, icy chills skittering up her arms.

"Let me make this clear," he said conversationally, as if they were just shooting the breeze in that silky—no, oily voice. "If you hurt my son, I'll have no choice. I'll have to hurt yours."

Chills turned into tremors and her hand shook uncontrollably, the portable phone trembling against her ear. "How do you know I have a son?"

"I know everything there is to know about you. Your multiple, shall we say, visits to the police station for prostitution. How far behind you are on your electric bill—it's going to be a hot summer, *Miz* Davis, if you don't tend to that. I know where Lincoln goes to school. As a matter of fact, he left your building about, oh, eight minutes ago."

Her throat constricted and she croaked, "Don't hurt my Lincoln."

Head swimming, she couldn't believe this nightmare. "He's all I have, please, leave him alone," she begged. "Senator, your son *did* try to kill me. Honest, he *did*. I'll remember his face until the day I die."

"I'm sure you were confused at the time with some brute trying to hurt you in a dark alley," he said in a placating tone. "Couldn't have been my boy, you see. He was with his lady friend all night. If you persist with your *story,* my boy will go to prison."

Indignation fired up her courage. "I know what I saw. The police said the car belonged to him. They showed me a picture and it's the same man who tried to kill me. I'm sorry if he's your son."

"I'm sorry, too," he replied as if defeated. "But...if you force me to visit my son in prison, you'll be forced to visit yours in the cemetery." The sheer malice in his voice convinced her that she spoke to the devil himself.

She gasped as the phone slipped out of her hand, bounced off her leg and landed in between two sofa cushions. Petrified to the core, she grasped it and shoved it against her ear again. "I'll do whatever you want," she said, hardly recognizing her own robotic voice.

"Excellent. I knew I'd help you sort this out." He reverted to that smarmy, conversational tone again, now more bone-chilling than ever. "And for all your inconvenience, I'm prepared to offer you a helping hand with your boy. It's very simple. If my boy goes free after you testify in court that he *isn't* the man who harmed you after all, your boy goes to college. Any college his abilities allow. You have my word. Do I have yours?"

Head downcast, her eyes streaming tears, she whispered, "You have my word."

****

Nauseous and light-headed, C. J. Demarco contemplated her opponent, dissecting each word of her opening statement. Clever, that the formidable State's Attorney herself represented the prosecution—two females at loggerheads over the credibility of a female prostitute. Photos of Shirlee Davis taken at hospital intake after the attack haunted Charlie, as did the tantalizing, assumed presence of Captain Patrick Sullivan behind her in the courtroom.

This distasteful case had robbed Charlie of too many things she held dear, Pat first and last. She hadn't called him but had wanted to twenty-four hours a day, even in dreams. Remembered love songs had played repetitively in her subconscious mind and her body literally ached for his touch. Her heart broke more each day when he hadn't called her, either, despite the fact that she had instigated her own exile from him.

Regrets the past month during Senator Morgan's impressive manipulation to speed up the wheels of justice had also whittled away at her conscience and had poked holes in her professional ethics. Exhausted from the sheer pace of pre-trial mechanics, she had lost her appetite, her existence reduced to a haze of eating and breathing the defense of the senator's son.

The familiar landscape of the courtroom as the focal point of justice seemed surreal to her now. Jackson Morgan III's word against the simple, seemingly honest Shirlee Davis'—that's what it boiled down to. The greater implications that her client might be a murderer twisted inside her, an agony of suspicions she constantly had suppressed, unable to function in her job otherwise.

During several pre-trial client consultations, she had grilled Morgan on the details of Shirlee's accusations but had never disproved what she still believed was a contrived, albeit unwavering alibi. Morgan's distasteful, slick personality, his hulking muscle-bound physicality and his air of entitled superiority had repeatedly repelled her.

But she couldn't fathom nor accept that he was the serial killer that the man she loved might believe him to be. *Pat.* How she yearned to quit the case, her financial troubles forgotten, and fly into Pat's sheltering arms. *If* Pat could ever want her again. Another serious doubt that this case had engendered.

Her trial face carefully plastered on, she rose to address the jury, adjusting her skirt sideways, since it swam on her now. Pat's certain attendance in the room was like a burning flame to her back.

"Ladies and gentlemen." She smiled into first one juror's eyes, and then several more in turn as she continued. "The defendant, Jackson Morgan III, did not attack Shirlee Davis that night as the prosecution claims. In fact, Mr. Morgan has never seen the plaintiff, Ms. Davis, until today in this courtroom. The defense will prove through testimony under oath that he was with his girlfriend all night, more than forty miles away from the dark alley during the time frame of the attack. Further, the defense will prove that police forensics cannot place the plaintiff in the defendant's car as she claims, having found no evidence during impound of the vehicle that supports her claim that she was a passenger in the car prior to the assault."

Pacing slowly in front of the jury box, she halted at its center. With a shrug of her shoulders, she widened her eyes and stated, "Actually, you will see that the police have found *no evidence at all* that the defendant committed the crimes charged against him by the State. I cannot speak to the motives of these false accusations on the part of the plaintiff, but the defense will prove beyond doubt that the accusations *are* false and that the defendant, Jackson Morgan III, is innocent. Thank you for your attention."

Charlie returned to her seat at the defense table registering Morgan's smug, pleased smile and derived no satisfaction from it. Sick at heart, for the first time in her career, Charlie desperately wanted to lose a case.

The State's Attorney rose in place, a blur in the corner of Charlie's left eye. "A brief recess, please? Ms. Davis just received word from the day camp's nurse that her son feels ill. She'd like to call and check on him" came the State's Attorney's request.

"Fifteen minutes," the judge declared.

Tracking Shirlee Davis' sluggish progress from behind the prosecutor's table and then past her toward the back of the courtroom, Charlie remained seated, pen in hand. *Just do your job. Listen. Try to figure out why she's lying...if she's lying. Just get this over with.*

Enveloped in Morgan's sugary, almost feminine-scented cologne, Charlie doodled on the pad. A tap on her shoulder from a heavy hand had her pulse spiking in anticipation. *Pat.*

Turning her head, her stomach fell.

"Couple sips of coffee before court reconvenes?" Jamie Freemont asked, offering her an insulated cup.

On a half smile and a shake of her head, Charlie declined. Turning away from Jamie, she glanced sideways and fixated on the hand Morgan rested on the table to her right. She had no difficulty imagining that powerful hand wrapped around Shirlee's neck, cutting off air...

The judge entered the courtroom through a paneled door behind the bench and the game was on again. The State's Attorney stood in front of her chair, folded hands hung against the hem of her suit jacket, facing the back of courtroom. "Check the ladies room, please?" she requested.

A female bailiff left the room, Charlie noted, attentive enough to dispense with doodling.

The bailiff returned and handed the State's Attorney an envelope, piquing Charlie's interest. A couple beats of silence as the prosecutor perused a letter and sighed, raising her head. "May counsel approach the bench, Judge?"

Furrowing her brow, Charlie jumped up and joined her opponent in front of the bench as the letter changed hands. The judge read it and muttered, "The State's witness claims the defendant is not her attacker. It appears the prosecution has no case. You may move to dismiss, C. J." She handed the letter to Charlie.

"That man at the table is not the man who attacked me. I will never forget that face and this isn't him. I'm very sorry but the picture the police showed me must have been bad. Tell him I'm sorry. Shirlee Davis."

"One minute, Judge," the prosecutor implored. "I can call officers to the stand who will corroborate her signed deposition that the attacker drove her to the scene of the attack in a Lotus with one of a kind vanity plates..."

"She obviously concocted the entire story," Charlie interjected. "There is no forensic evidence that she was a passenger in that car. Even to the contrary, she's dropped the charges against my client with respect to battery and attempted murder."

"Exactly," the judge added bluntly. "Move back, Counselors."

The buzz of muted conversations in the courtroom while they had conferred at the bench heightened as Charlie returned to her place and stood facing front.

The judge's gavel cracked, soliciting silence. "The plaintiff has dropped all charges against the defendant. Case dismissed. Mr. Morgan, you're free to leave."

Speechless, Charlie stood frozen to the spot.

Staring over Charlie's head at the audience whose protests echoed, the judge bellowed, "I want this courtroom cleared *now.*"

Feet shuffled and scuffed the floor, the door banged on its hinges occasionally as the crowd exited the courtroom. Confused and insulted by her central role in this mess, Charlie didn't dare turn around to single out Pat and focused only on collecting her things from the defense tabletop, repacking her briefcase.

She smelled Senator Morgan's approach, a spicy aftershave aroma that preceded the jarring clap on her shoulder. "Excellent work, little lady. I'll make sure Fremont gives you a well deserved raise for taking care of my son."

Squinting up at the senator, Charlie forcefully bit her tongue before responding. "You give me false credit, sir. Obviously, this was a case of mistaken identity as you originally told me."

"Exactly." Morgan administered a shoulder clap to his son, a literal smack that sounded like it stung. "I'll be in the car out front." The senator winked, a baffling gesture to Charlie, turned on his heel and strode out of the courtroom. All that was missing was a round of "Hail To The Chief."

"Miss Demarco, may I call you Charlotte? Or do you prefer C. J.?" His voice was dull, lifeless, none of the music of the good ole boy in his tone like his old man's.

Charlie couldn't read Jackson Morgan's strange expression, either, and didn't see the next coming, "I want to be on a first name basis when we have dinner together tonight," he declared, clearly a demand. "Later, perhaps, I can thank you...properly. For your services."

Now his expression spoke loud and clear, the unspeakable letch. Throwing her head back, she burst into laughter. Then, straight-faced, she glared directly into his creepy, empty eyes and injected utter conviction in her response. "Don't call me anything. Don't ever call me again."

Charlie continued, outraged, unperturbed by the malicious glint in his eyes, "I don't know what you and your *father* pulled to silence this woman for his *boy's* and his own reputation's sake, but I'm not fooled for an instant. I wouldn't have dinner with you under any circumstances, little man."

He might have sputtered a protest—a strangled sound clearly issued from his direction, but she didn't care, having already presented her back to him with the sincere hope she'd never have to look at him again. Her hand, a death grip on her briefcase handle, she hauled it with a thump against her side and propelled forward up the aisle in agitated retreat.

She'd find Pat. Nothing else mattered.

Chapter 15

"Check out Shirlee Davis' apartment and the son's day camp. She bolted after opening arguments. Thanks." Patrick pocketed his phone.

Frustrated and pissed beyond memory, he slouched against the building, hurting in every way. In the shadow of the marble column, he remained invisible to Charlie as she emerged from the courthouse. Blood surged through his body, pounding in his head. *How could I have been so wrong about a person?*

Charlie—the source of the piercing pain in his heart and an affront to his values upholding the law.

Losing to the defense on a technicality was abhorrent, especially if the technicality pointed to police error. But the defense tampered with a witness? A crime. An unforgivable miscarriage of justice.

Shirlee Davis had refused to make eye contact with Patrick when she had rushed past him in the courtroom. More disturbing to him, she had looked frightened. Now he knew why.

Someone had gotten to her. How? Had to be a threat, or a payoff.

Could the woman he loved stoop that low? He gazed at Charlie's slim profile, her straight back. Her suit hid her sensual figure and the bun concealed her long, wild mane of hair as if her courtroom costume transformed a warm, loving, playful woman into a heartless, sterile, win-at-all-costs machine.

Who are you, Charlie? Professionally, he had

concurred that the case presented a conflict of interest. But the impersonal, damned note she had sent still galled him—especially the *Love, Charlie* signature.

What a snow job.

Refusing to delve further into his misguided feelings for her, he had focused relentlessly on compiling evidence against Morgan instead.

A waste of time. He had come up empty solving the case. The whirlwind rush to trial hadn't allowed him to draw any conclusions from the lack of new Garbage Man murder victims, either. He had relied on the Morgan conviction and imprisonment to test those conclusions, buy more time.

And Charlie's to blame for undermining me? He had always been an unerring judge of character. A woman couldn't have scrambled his brain enough to alter that. He had to have the facts. His gut told him that Charlie couldn't be behind Shirlee Davis' stunning reversal, but if she played the slightest part in this...

Reporters waved microphones near Charlie's face.

"Ms. De Marco! Ms. De Marco! Senator Morgan is calling for the resignation of Captain Patrick Sullivan. Do you agree with the senator?"

Patrick grimaced. *Son of a bitch.*

Her face an emotionless mask, Charlie veered sideways, in motion to bypass the crowd of reporters.

"Shirlee Davis is a prostitute, isn't she? Aren't you furious that the police believed her instead of an innocent man?" one of the group shouted.

Charlie halted in front of a young blonde reporter, an aggressive stance nearly nose to nose with the journalist. "Ms. Davis was understandably confused when the police showed her a picture of Senator Morgan's son. She had just been brutally attacked. How would you feel if you were almost killed? Could you think straight?"

The reporter stepped back as Charlie continued, "This is an unfortunate case of mistaken identity. Mr. Morgan is an innocent man and justice was served today. Leave Ms. Davis alone. Her attacker is still at large. Focus on that and support the police in apprehending him."

"Do you agree with the senator that Captain Sullivan should be fired?'

Patrick strained to hear Charlie's response.

"No, I don't," she declared. "Captain Sullivan's department had to arrest my client based on the victim's identification. I'm sure he'll reopen the case and find Ms. Davis's attacker. I have complete faith in the Chicago police force."

Bullshit. We had her attacker and you know it. You got him off. Patrick yanked his cell phone out of his jacket pocket and texted Charlie. *We need to talk. Meet me at the swan boats at Lincoln Park.*

Patrick observed Charlie grab the phone off her waistband and study the screen. Squinting in the bright sunshine, she shaded her eyes with a hand and scanned the vicinity.

Senator Morgan bellowed, "Little lady!" beckoning her to the bottom of the stairs where he held court amid another cluster of microphone-toting humanity.

She frowned but stomped down the stairs towards the senator and his son, trailing reporters behind her.

Clipping the phone back on her waistband without answering the text message, a phony smile plastered on her face, she joined the group at the bottom of the stairs.

Patrick punched the column. Pain shot up his arm. Ignoring it, he skirted the column and slipped into the building bound for the back exit.

****

"Here's the little lady now." The senator wrapped his arm around Charlie's shoulders. Unable to remove it with any degree of grace, she stood rigid between the senator and her sneering client. Training her eyes upward toward the courthouse doors, she hoped to catch a glimpse of Pat.

Where are you?

"Ms. De Marco is one of the best lawyers in Chicago," the politician proclaimed.

"It's easy to defend an innocent man," Charlie tossed out, ready to escape, but the senator tightened the grip on her shoulder.

"Tomorrow, my office will begin an investigation into the conduct and methods of the Chicago police force. The new captain is too inexperienced to handle the responsibilities of the job."

Despite the heat of the sun, involuntary chills coursed through Charlie. *Oh, Pat, this is so unfair. This man is beyond reprehensible. I detest that I'm involved with him.*

"Are you going to ask for Captain Sullivan's resignation?" An evening network news correspondent shouted.

"I'll not comment further until my office completes the investigation. But I will promise the good people of Chicago that upstanding innocent citizens like my son will not be treated with disrespect by law enforcement authorities. I will hold the police force responsible. Thank you for your support. Have a good evening."

The senator tugged Charlie towards his waiting limo. "Come out to dinner with us to celebrate."

Determined to remain impassive exposed to the media reps, she gritted her teeth and forced civility into her response, "Thank you, Senator, I would like to join you, but I have an appointment. Enjoy your evening."

****

Patrick leaned back. The slats of the wooden bench creaked in protest. *Damn it. I thought she might come.*

He should have gone back to his office to deal with the fallout from the case, give up on her permanently. But he wanted, no needed, to hear Charlie deny any knowledge of witness manipulation.

His stomach churned while he punched numbers on his cell phone pad, listened to a couple rings until the answering click.

"Sergeant Lucas."

"Josh, I'm glad you're on duty."

"Hey, Captain. What the hell happened? The press is everywhere and the superintendent is looking for you. Are the rumors true? Did Morgan walk?"

"The witness dropped the charges apparently in a note after she left court on a pretense. Turn the television on," Patrick said, looking at his watch. "...and in about a half hour, you'll see the State's Attorney with egg on her face."

"Ah, fuck," Lucas declared.

Couldn't have said it better myself. "Now you know why the superintendent wants to see me. I'll be back in the office in a little while. I want you to set up surveillance."

"On the senator's son?"

"No, we have to steer clear of the Morgans for now. Set up surveillance of the alley where Shirlee was attacked. I want that homeless person who helped her."

"Will do, sir."

Patrick clicked off. His call-waiting signal had sounded repetitively during the entire conversation with Lucas, but he hadn't picked up.

The missed call display that listed his brothers', sister's and parents' telephone numbers prompted a smile. *The Sullivans are circling the wagons. Guess I made the five o'clock news.*

He chuckled in spite of the sinking dread in his stomach. His eyes lit on the super's duplicate office numbers on the list. Seven calls but not the one that counted.

Pocketing the phone, he rested on the bench. Families strolled around the pond where a few swan boats glided along the water. Giggling children ran around carefree and enjoyed the waning summer afternoon. The smell of hot pretzels and popcorn triggered stomach growls. He hadn't eaten anything since dinner last night; the adrenaline over the assumed successful outcome of the trial had suppressed physical hunger. The only hunger he had experienced last night—the past month—was for Charlie.

I'm wasting my time. She's not coming. It's over. Conflict of interest, my ass. Maybe it's better this way.

He rose and ambled towards the sidewalk where he had parked his car. Charlie leaned against a tree in the shade, two bottles of water in her hands, staring back at him.

"I didn't think you were coming," Patrick remarked.

****

None of the appealing gentleness shone in his sky blue eyes. Where was that spark of delight at seeing at her that she had come to relish?

"I wasn't," Charlie improvised. "This is probably a mistake." She held out one of the bottles.

He took it, twisted the cap and took a long swallow. She drank, too, for something to do with her hands. The cool water soothed her suddenly dry throat.

Recapping his bottle, he said, "Thanks."

"You're welcome." She noticed the swollen

knuckle on his hand and pointed to it. "What happened to your hand?"

"It's nothing."

Charlie trudged over to the bench that Pat had vacated and sat down with a sigh.

"What did you want to talk to me about?" She closed her eyes.

He sat next to her, close enough that their legs touched and his thigh muscle twitched and stiffened. Reading the body language, she adjusted her seat on the bench and inched away, the last thing she wanted to do.

Obviously irritated, he blurted, "How did you do it?"

"What?"

"How did you convince Shirlee to lie? What did you do to her?"

Her eyes flew open, took in the stubborn set of his jaw. "What are you insinuating? I didn't do anything. I'm shocked she refused to testify against my client." Charlie scrubbed her hands across her face.

"You expect me to believe that?" Pat slapped his hand against the bench.

Charlie jerked at the loud noise. "I don't care if you believe me or not. Look, I shouldn't have come."

With a heave of her chest, she shifted to stand and run away from this awful rejection. *I deserve this retaliation. I didn't explain when I rejected him.*

He grasped her wrist. "Don't go."

Unsteady, she remained inert on the bench, lacking the energy to defend against his suspicions and allowed his huge hand to remain circled around her wrist.

"Are you eating or sleeping? You look tired and your wrist is just a bone."

Charlie yanked her arm away from his hold. "Where is this going? You're suddenly concerned about my health?"

Shaking his head he said, "I need the facts about what happened in the courtroom this afternoon."

She sighed. "Yeah, me, too."

"Oh, come on, Counselor. How do you live with yourself? Is winning really that important to you?"

His sarcastic inflection insulted her and spiked her pulse. "You don't know me at all. Yes, winning is important to me. Tell me it's not important to you. But I'd never..."

"Who got to Shirlee Davis?" His voice rose.

Facing him now, her eyes narrowed to slits and she responded, "Has it occurred to you that you arrested an innocent man and that you acted too quickly on a shaky ID?"

"Answering with a question. Typical C. J. Demarco," he declared. His flat tone, his dispassionate expression, tore her in two.

"Maybe your department *is* inept," she jabbed, not even slightly intimidated by the ominous darkening in his eyes.

"We both know that's not true. I'll prove he's guilty."

"Good luck with that. Senator Morgan will never let you near his son again."

"Maybe." His stare held no trace of the seductive, passionate lover she had missed. "Just tell me you had no knowledge of witness tampering. I have to hear it from you."

Charlie's heart twisted, crushed that he could suspect this of her. She sprang up, determined to conceal that he had the power to hurt her. "Goodbye, Pat."

"I thought we had something between us," he said, his tone strident. "You at least owe me an honest answer."

She bent her head. "We did." Unable to stem them, compromising tears tracked down her cheeks.

"I had *nothing* to do with what happened in court today."

His eyes softened. "Okay, then." He reached for her but she evaded his hand.

"Don't." Stepping back, she swiped the tears away with the back of her hand.

"Charlie, you're not being fair."

"You're being fair to me?" Anger bubbled in her voice. "The law's always *fair*, Patrick."

"You have to appreciate my position. Wouldn't you question me, too, if you were in my shoes?"

I won't grace that with an answer. She turned and strode a couple steps away.

"Charlie, despite everything, I love you," he said to her back.

A spear of pain shot straight through her core. Pivoting on the spot, eyes huge, she declared with her last ounce of pride, "Apparently you think all's fair in love, Captain. Goodbye."

Chapter 16

Patrick stared at Charlie's back as she
disappeared around the corner, his head swimming
with regret. Inclined to slam his fist again, this time
into a nearby tree, he stewed. Once Jackson Morgan
was back behind bars where he belonged, he would
somehow sort this out with her.

His cell phone chirped and he answered without
looking at the caller ID display. "Sullivan."

"Sir. We have the homeless man."

His heart skipped a beat, hopeful. "Finally, some
good news today."

"Not exactly good news, sir. We found him in the
Dumpster with his head bashed in."

"Ah, fuck." He kneaded his temple.

"Yessir. We're fucked."

In motion toward his car, Patrick said, "I'm on
my way to the superintendent's office before going
off duty. I'll be in at 0700 tomorrow."

The car bucked with his heavy-footed taps on
the brakes navigating the congested city street. In
no particular hurry to face his superior, traffic
conditions aggravated him anyway. The aching band
of tension tightened around his head with each
forward lurch of the car.

Responding to an incoming call by punching the
Bluetooth button on the wheel, Patrick grunted,
"Yes."

"Saw you on TV, bro," Brian Sullivan remarked.

"Huh," he responded. "Pride of the Sullivan
family."

"The senator is blowing a lot of wind. Is Morgan

really innocent?" Brian asked.

"No." Patrick slammed on the brakes to avoid a car's rear bumper just in time. "He's the perp. Somebody got to the witness."

"It's a shit storm, all right. But don't let it get to you."

You don't know the half of it. "When the boss is through with me, I'll see if it gets to me or not." Chuckling, he shook his head.

"When you're done downtown, how about some three B's?"

Beer, barbecue and basketball—the summertime cure-all for Sullivan boys' ills. Despite his bleak situation, Patrick brightened at the prospect. "Sounds good. Joe's house?"

"Nope, Kay's..."

The import of an invitation to their sister's house hung between them. "Really? How did you guys manage to persuade her?"

"It was her idea. The women are out grocery shopping now." Brian's voice quivered.

At a standstill at a light, Patrick bowed his head. *Kay must really think I'm a class A screw-up. But bless my soul, she's doing this for me.* "I'll be there as soon as I can."

****

The sight of his brothers sweating bare-chested beneath the hoop in Kay's driveway, showboating for Kay's neighbors as usual, swelled his heart. On a lazy jog from his car parked at the curb, Patrick unbuttoned his dress shirt, slipped it off and tossed it in the grass.

"Two on two," he declared, blocking Danny's pass to Joe with an easy upward sweep of his arm.

"Joe, you team with Pat," Danny dictated. "One eye evens out his extra two-inch height advantage."

Joe shot Danny a murderous glare with his "one eye," but sauntered over to Patrick. "Care to put some money where that big mouth is, Dan?"

Danny dribbled the ball in place, grinning widely, as Patrick stepped in front of him in a defensive stance and Joe covered Brian. Pound, pound, the ball hit the pavement. "Made a call a few minutes ago," Danny said. Pound, pound, pound.

Patrick eyed the pumping ball in Danny's hand.

"To a friend of mine..." Danny continued.

Used to his brother's ploys, Patrick listened with half an ear and focused on the dribbling motion of the ball. With a grunt, Danny swung a one-handed pass sideways to Brian who veered right and away from Joe's arm swipe to catch it.

The rhythmic pounding resumed as Brian dribbled in place and toyed with Joe. Patrick stretched his arms wide in front of his brother and focused on Danny's green eyes for a tell of his next offensive move.

"I'm trying to arrange a tail on Morgan through Lake Forest PD. Figured you'd want to keep an eye on him. I may not be able to pull it off with the heat. But it's worth a try," Danny said.

"Thanks." Patrick's gratitude relaxed his defenses enough for Danny's opportunistic fake left, surge right. A couple flying lopes to position under the hoop and Dan nudged Brian's pass into the basket.

"Shit," Joe proclaimed with a disgusted glance at Patrick. "You're really off your game, little brother."

Joe swung an arm around Patrick's shoulder. "Let's bag this and eat."

Amid the collective thunder of tramping sizes fourteen to sixteen feet, Patrick accompanied his brothers into Kay's home. The stab of grief encountering the assembly of chattering Sullivans in her cheerful kitchen nearly undid him. *God, I miss you, Jimmy and Mike.*

The music of women's laughter, Kay's most magical of all, stopped abruptly as they caught sight of Patrick—the dubious man of the moment. All eyes on him, he uttered a simple, "Hi, everybody."

Kay hustled over and pecked him on the cheek with a smile.

"Hi, sis." He swept her into a deep hug. "Where are all the kids?"

Arching her neck, Kay gazed at his face, her eyes clear, her cheeks glowed a healthier color. "Over in Dan and Molly's pool. Mikey's in charge. Also, Mary and Amy are certified junior lifeguards now."

Kay beamed a smile at him and he grinned back, remembering the story of Jimmy's near drowning that he had related to Charlie on a windy pier—missing Jimmy—missing Charlie.

Still holding his arms around her, Patrick peered at the adults over the crown of Kay's head. "Whoa, family powwow?"

"We want to help you. Sit with Daddy," Kay suggested.

John Sullivan patted the seat of a kitchen chair and Patrick eased into it. "Hi, son. Rough day." John's lips twisted in a lopsided smile.

Patrick snorted. "You could say that, Pop. O'Halloran's backing me, though. It'll blow over."

"Well, he better," John, the ex-commissioner, opined. "You going to do something official about the witness tampering?"

"Yes, but I'm still working on the doing something part."

Noisy scrapes along the floor as Danny, Joe and Brian pulled chairs up to the table.

"Have some nachos," Kay offered as she slid a heaping plate into the center of the table.

His brothers dug in and chomped while Patrick abstained. As if reading his mind, Bobbie tossed him a can of beer. Pastel sunshine through the kitchen window highlighted Bobbie's hair, a shade so similar to his they could be siblings by blood instead of marriage. He couldn't love her more if they were. *The same goes for the other Sullivan women.* A wave of sadness crested inside him at Charlie's absence at the barbecue, excluded from the Sullivan women, from his life.

Maybe forever.

Popping the top and swigging the cold brew, Patrick related, "The witness has already rabbited. Her apartment's empty and the landlord claimed an envelope under his door contained rent through the end of the lease, no forwarding address." He gulped more beer. "There was a witness to her attack in the alley that night, a vagrant. We couldn't put a net around him before the trial started. Didn't think we had to with the victim's testimony, but the victim *is* a prostitute. We always had problems with credibility—not that adding a bum would have greatly enhanced the case."

Laughter rang in Kay's kitchen again. Delighted at the sheer normalcy after all they'd been through recently, Patrick actually enjoyed being the "butt of the joke."

"Anyway," he continued, "the bum just turned up in an alley with a bashed head and no pulse. I learned that after I more or less accused Charlie of witness tampering."

A chorus of female reprisals ensued.

"What!"

"Oh, Pat!"

"You're kidding!" The women fluttered to the table like a swarm of angry butterflies.

Cowed, his cheeks burned. "I had to hear her deny it." He surged to his feet and paced behind the chairs on his side of the table. "I had so much at stake with this case."

"I'm confused," Joe declared.

"Me, too," Bobbie professed. "You're questioning Charlie's ethics in an assault case when your witness failed to testify against her client? Seems like the victim had the most at stake."

"The victim didn't know it, but I'm certain she's the only woman who's survived to identify the Garbage Man Murderer," Patrick said bluntly.

Gasps and then dead silence. A couple seconds passed before their questions peppered him.

"You're certain?"

"How do you know?"

"Do you have evidence?"

"Why didn't you charge him?"

Patrick stood still and huffed a sigh. "Shirlee Davis *should* have testified that Morgan carried a baseball bat in his car. The serial murderer violated each victim post-mortem with a bat. We've withheld that fact from the press. Morgan didn't use the bat on her and during the short time preceding the trial we couldn't scrape up one material fact to charge him with the serial murders. I relied on the Davis trial to jail him and at least enter the bat's possession into court records. Minimally, we'd get him off the street and stop the killings. He's free now and—"

"I'll put more pressure on Lake Forest to follow Morgan round the clock," Danny offered.

"Hell, I'll tail him myself," Joe declared.

"Me, too," Brian echoed.

"Thanks, but it would only make me feel worse if I brought you down with me. One Sullivan career on the line is more than enough. Senator Morgan has to be responsible at least for bribing a witness. Maybe worse," Patrick reasoned. "He's untouchable and I don't know the extent of his willingness to protect his son. If I'm right about the serial murders *and* the senator knows what his son's about, we have two monsters to apprehend."

Shaking his head, Patrick admitted, "I took my frustration out on Charlie since she obviously jumped to Senator Morgan's commands. Problem is I'm not sure how high."

Matty rushed to him and clasped his hands. "Patrick, listen to me." Her soulful eyes held his. "She might be a pawn in this man's wrongdoing but she would *never* knowingly abuse the law. There's more to Charlie than meets the eye. I'm very attuned to her generous heart. I see tremendous sweetness and sensitivity under the surface with her."

"Yeah, well, I made her cry," Patrick said, bitterness sour on his tongue. "But she's a pretty talented actress on stage and in court."

"I like Charlie very much. We all do," his mother attested. "I think she's a genuinely good person."

"Yes," his father seconded.

I am a class A screw-up. "I'm glad," Patrick said, surprising himself and flabbergasting his parents, judging from the astonished expressions on their faces. "Because the last thing I said to her before she stalked away from me in a huff was that I love her."

"Mother of God," Joe exclaimed. "Could this be any more...?"

Jean Sullivan's piercing gaze in Joe's direction curtailed further conjecture from her son.

Turning crystal blue eyes on Patrick, Jean declared, "Well, then, Patrick, it's understandable if the woman thinks you have a very strange way of showing it.

****

Bright white light flickered in the dark room. He hunched forward in his seat on the hassock in front of the television. White knuckled, he gripped the remote control.

Damn you, you smug bitch. You will be sorry you

ever laughed at me.

C. J. Demarco's voice filled the room. "It's easy to defend an innocent man."

He rewound the tape and she repeated, "It's easy to defend an innocent man."

Again. "It's easy to defend an innocent man." Her voice, once appealing to him, bounced off the walls, echoing.

A grunt in the corner of the room distracted him. "Shut the fuck up," he commanded.

A short windup and he pitched the remote into the television screen full force. Glass splintered as the set imploded. Pungent fumes stung his nostrils heightening his fury.

You won't get away with this. He yanked the black suit jacket off the chair-back, slipped it on and tugged at the sleeves. *A little short but it will do.*

Stuffing a hand in its pocket, he pulled out a crumbled pack of cigarettes and a butane lighter.

"You really shouldn't smoke. It will kill you." His deep, maniacal laughter echoed as he rolled a sheet of newspaper and flicked the lighter wheel. Igniting the paper, he brandished the flaming torch.

A rope-bound man lay on the floor next to the couch, struggling against his restraints and grunting animal sounds behind gray electrical tape plastered over his mouth. His eyes widened in horror as his captor methodically set anything flammable in sight on fire: first the curtains, a bunch of papers that served as kindling for the wooden desk, the chintz-covered hassock and then the skirt of the couch's upholstery. Acrid, black smoke snaked up the walls and billowed closer to the man's prone body as the flames blazed brighter, higher.

Sneering he knelt and almost gently tipped the edges of the bound man's pants with the flaming newspaper until the fire took hold.

Tossing the torch on the cotton rug beneath the

writhing man, he pronounced, "You don't have to take orders from the *senator* anymore." He guffawed. *Ah, the irony.* "Goodbye, Jackson Morgan the third."

Covering his mouth with his hand, he hurried toward the door, the inferno a searing heat trailing him out of the room. Without a backward glance, he slammed the door.

Chapter 17

Disappointed, Emily Demarco recorded her message on Charlie's cell phone, "Hi, sweetie. Call me as soon as you pick up this message. Fantastic news! Hurry up. Call me."

Laughing, she snapped her phone shut, turned and walked straight into Wolf Man's hairy chest. "Oops! Sorry, Jeff."

The tall man grinned affably, a weird contrast to his "menacing monster" stage makeup. "Great show today, Em. You were on fire. The crowd loved you."

"Thanks. It felt great today." Passing him in the narrow, backstage hallway, she proceeded to the closet-sized room designated as her dressing room; its only saving grace, a tiny porthole window that afforded some natural light.

Near bursting with elation, Emily wanted to shout her secret from the stage. Superstitious, like many actors, she wouldn't tell a soul until she shared it with Charlie first. Since Charlie had always had faith that she deserved the lead in *Parkview Life*, Emily needed to tell Charlie the news to believe it all real. This morning her agent had notified her that she had the coveted part! And that she'd fax a contract to her right about now.

Glancing at her watch, Emily determined she still had two hours before the next show. *If I hurry, I can make it to the condo and back and see it in writing. Better sign that contract fast before the producer changes his mind. Maybe Charlie will be home by the time I get there and I can tell her in person. Ask her for a quick review of the paperwork.*

Delighted that she had excellent, *free,* legal counsel in her adored sister—delighted in general, she angled an arm over her shoulder and tugged on the zipper. An expert at the quick change, she shed her costume and slipped into comfortable jeans and a sleeveless, cotton shirt in seconds.

Absorbed in excited thought, she jumped at the sound of a man's deep voice. "Miss Demarco."

"Yes." Her body tensed as she faced the tall, muscular man clad in a black suit, white shirt and black tie.

The dark wraparound sunglasses he wore concealed his eyes and added to his threatening appearance. He marched into the tiny room flipping open a leather wallet as he drew closer to her. The sun's rays through her little porthole sparkled off the shiny shield inside.

"Agent Dixon, Miss Demarco. I need you to come with me." His large hand clasped her elbow.

"Why? I don't understand." Cornered and trembling, she shook off his hand and backed into the chair, almost stumbling.

"I didn't do anything wrong," Emily declared, heat rising in her cheeks.

"You need to come with me for your own protection. Miss C. J. Demarco sent me. There have been threats on her life."

Emily's heart seized. "Oh God, no! Is my sister all right?"

"Yes, miss. I'm with Senator Morgan's security detail and he's arranged her protection. She refused custody unless we protected you, too."

Placing a hand over her heart, Emily sighed, relieved. *So like Charlie. Always taking care of me.*

"My orders are to bring you to her so we can keep you both safe. Come with me." He grabbed her elbow again and led her out of the dressing room.

Half jogging next to him to keep pace with his

broad strides, she stifled a protest at his too tight grip on her arm. *In his line of work, he probably doesn't appreciate his own strength.*

"I just tried to call my sister, but she didn't answer," Emily commented.

"No, miss, we wouldn't allow her to use her cell phone," he said, his voice a flat monotone. "In fact, I need to confiscate your cell phone, too. Are you aware there is a tracking device in all cell phones?"

"You are kidding me." Emily stopped short, suffering a brief, painful arm tug until he halted, too.

"I don't kid, miss." He extended his arm in her direction, palm up.

Obediently, she dug her phone out of her bag and handed it over.

Uneasy with this stoic guardian, but desperate to get to Charlie, Emily slid into the back seat of the town car. He closed the back door to her right and her heart skittered. The blackened windows caged her like she was no longer a part of the normal world. The driver's door opened and the agent sat behind the wheel. A thumping click sounded as he locked the doors.

****

Charlie slumped against the cushions of the sofa in her condo, cocooned in the softness. Her bare feet tucked under her, she stared at her reflection in the sliding doors, Lake Michigan a panoramic, blue-green sea beyond the glass. A baggy pair of sweatpants hid the shape of her legs and a black-and-blue plaid flannel shirt hung loosely around her hips. Her dark, curly hair fell in wild tangles around her shoulders. Guilt pinched a little that she had blown off work and stayed home today, a virtual couch potato. But she needed a mental health day.

Too much had happened in the last few weeks. Although not always happy with her job and the demands it placed on her, she had remained content slaving for dollars determined to keep her stint at the firm temporary. When she replaced all the money her parents had lost, she would be free to choose how she earned her living in the future.

Was a life defending criminals the right choice for her? She doubted that she could continue winning cases for people that she knew in her heart should be behind bars.

Her phone beeped, signaling yet another voice mail. She had lost count of Jamie's concerned messages. Since she had started at Schotz, Pearson and Freemont, she had never missed a day of work. A bout of walking pneumonia last year hadn't kept her away from her desk. But today, debilitated by heart sickness, she just couldn't face the job.

Pat had accused her of tampering with a witness. How dare he impugn her reputation? Despite the character of most of her clients, *her* honest reputation had always been above reproach.

The television in the living room had provided background noise all morning, a series of mindless game shows and soap operas. She glanced at the screen. *He's cute.*

Some soap opera hunk begged some tall blonde actress, "Please don't leave me. I need you."

"I don't care what you need, Brock. I don't need you." The cool blonde's casual delivery struck Charlie as heartless.

Tears filled Charlie's eyes. *Brock, I know how you feel. I need Pat but he apparently doesn't need me.* She raised the remote control and pointed it at the television. *Enough of the pity party. Get a grip.*

"We interrupt regular programming with a breaking news story." The screen displayed the chiseled, solemn face of a local television reporter. "I'm standing across the street from a townhouse owned by Senator Morgan where a fire broke out about two hours ago." The camera panned back. Fire hoses snaked in the street and dense plumes of dark smoke billowed out all the windows of the two-story building. Water gushed in the gutter.

The camera cut back to the reporter's face. "Fire Chief Cushna has informed Channel 7 News that the fire has been contained. A body believed to be Senator Jackson Morgan's son, Jackson Morgan III, was removed from the building moments ago. The victim's body will be transported to the county morgue. Senator Morgan is said to be en route to the morgue and will issue a statement after viewing the body. Channel 7 News will carry the press conference live. Stay tuned to your local station. We return you to your regular programming already in progress."

After muting the television Charlie dug deep between the cushions and located her cell phone. *I shouldn't have ignored those last couple calls from Jamie.*

She listened to the two new messages her boss had left requesting her to call in, so he'd be assured that she was okay. Then she smiled when she heard her sister's melodic voice. "Hurry up. Call me," Emi chimed, followed by her infectious laugh.

I could use some good news, Em. Charlie tapped her sister's phone number on the keypad anxious to hear all about...whatever... Her boss could wait.

"Hello," a man answered.

"Oh, I'm sorry. I must have dialed the wrong number." Confused, Charlie stared at the phone display: *Connected Emi's Cell.*

Ready to click off and redial anyway the man rasped through the phone, "No, *bitch*, you called the right number."

Charlie's fingers froze over the keypad, her heart lurching in her chest. "I want to speak to Emily Demarco." Her voice cracked.

"Guess what? I don't give a shit what you want. It's what I want that matters." Her icy fingers gripped the phone to her ear as she frantically searched her memory to identify the familiar voice.

Panic expanded in her chest, her erratic heartbeat drumming in her ears. "Tell me what you want. Anything. Just don't hurt my sister," Charlie pleaded.

****

Patrick raised his shoulder, propping the phone to his ear, and focused on the computer screen in front of him. He scanned the news flash as he waited for the call to go through. Several rings and a click. Charlie's recorded voice sounded in his ear, the prelude to the beep signal to record his message. *Is she watching the same news broadcast now? How is she reacting to the news about her client? Will she even return my call?*

"Hi, this is Pat. When you grab this message, give me a call."

A hush fell over the squad room as the consequences of the fire apparently sank in. His men would never celebrate death, not even Morgan's, but judging from their grinning faces they shared his relief that the Garbage Man Murder spree was now over. Maybe they'd never prove that Jackson Morgan III was the deranged killer, but that was the consensus in his squad room.

The cell phone vibrated across the cluttered desk. He glanced at the caller ID and experienced a burst of happiness. *She'll talk to me at least.*

"Hi. You heard the news about Morgan. Charlie I want to…"

"Pat, please, please, help me! I don't know who else to call!" Charlie's hysteria blasted in his ear. Her anguished sobbing stabbed directly into his heart.

"Of course, I'll help. What's wrong?" No response

156

except irregular breathing and high-pitched sounds. "Try to be calm, Charlie, and tell me what you need." No answer as his alarm increased. "Sweetheart, what do you need me to do? I'd do anything for you."

"He has her. He has Emily."

"Who?"

"Jackson Morgan."

"The senator?" Patrick rubbed his hand over the stubble on his chin and closed his eyes concentrating on the nature of her problem.

"No, his son kidnapped my sister!" she wailed. "Oh...Pat..."

"No, sweetheart. It's someone else. He died in a fire a few hours ago." Patrick stuffed folders into the desk drawer, clearing off his desk. Charlie needed him and he'd go to her.

"I have the news on now. I don't care what they are reporting," she stated, her voice marginally stronger. "He just answered my sister's cell phone. I don't know who they dragged out of the fire, but I guarantee you it wasn't Morgan. You have to believe me."

"I do and I'm on my way." He flipped the switch for the overhead lights off. "Are you at the office?"

"No, I'm home."

"I'll be right there."

"Pat..." She paused, her erratic breathing like a wind in his ear. "Thank you."

"Anything for you, princess." He disconnected the phone.

Winding through the desks in the squad room he barked out orders. "Lucas put an APB out on Jackson Morgan III."

"Captain, he's in the morgue," one of his men called out. "It's all over the news."

"I have information that he's not the corpse. Morgan kidnapped Emily Demarco, C. J. Demarco's twin. Check for cell phone records under Emily's name. Call the coroner's office and have them check the dental records on the body. Don't rely on the senator's ID. Call me."

Patrick sprinted down the hall, out of the building to the parking lot.

"Captain," Lucas hollered holding open the station house door. "Your sister-in-law is on line one."

"Ask her to call me on my cell."

Lucas nodded and disappeared inside the building.

Chapter 18

Sirens blaring, bubble light swirling strobes, Patrick careened into lunchtime traffic in the city. The speedometer edged toward ninety as he maneuvered his way through the cabs and buses like a professional NASCAR driver. He clipped on his earpiece and answered his cell.

"Sullivan."

"Hi. Pat…"

"Hi, Matty," he interrupted her bluntly. "I'm in the middle of something. Can I call you back?" Sweat trickled down the back of his shirt.

"I'm calling to help. I received a truth. Charlie's in grave danger," she blurted out.

"Sorry. I'm listening."

"I saw Charlie lying on a floor."

"You saw her sister, Emily," he contradicted her, his tone gentle.

"Okay. They look so much alike. Emily is terrified. Her teeth rattle and her body shakes constantly. Her hands are tied in front of her. She's on the floor below a window. You know I don't always understand what I hear or see, Pat, and this sounds odd, I know. Maybe too odd to mention…"

Patrick hung on every word. Her truths had helped his brothers solve two cases. He'd accept any insight that Matty could offer. "Please, Matty. Anything may help."

"I saw a totem pole. Huge, elaborately carved, authentic. There's a sign on the lower portion of the pole. It reads, Lily's Dream Two, like the number. I have no clue where it is in relation to Emily. I hope this can identify her location somehow. I promise I'll call if I have anything else that might help."

Instinctively, he anticipated her cutting off conversation. "Wait, sis, don't hang up yet."

She chuckled. "Technically, I'm not your sister-in-law yet, no less your sister. Although I told your man I was your sister-in-law to get through as soon as I could. I hope you don't mind."

Patrick smiled, maneuvering the squad car into the labyrinth-like parking garage adjacent to Charlie's building. "Thank you for calling me. And, you should refer to yourself as my sister, Matty. If you're crazy enough to follow through with marrying Brian, then you're certainly crazy enough to be a full-fledged Sullivan."

"Aw, thanks, Pat. I think." She chuckled and then the line went dead.

I don't understand yet what Matty's vision means, but it is true. Matty Connors soon-to-be Sullivan is never wrong.

****

The elevator doors swished open when he reached Charlie's floor. She stood in the hall near the door of her condo, probably had remained in the same place since he had left the station house, waiting for him. Her face, a mask of torment, tore at his heart. Wearing shapeless sweat pants and a man-sized flannel shirt, her black hair uncombed in a riot of curls, she still stunned him with her beauty. Wild-eyed, she raced down the hallway into his arms.

Squeezing her tight for a moment brought him a sense of peace and soothed an ache he hadn't acknowledged until just holding her temporarily banished it.

"Let's go inside," he suggested, leading her through the doorway and over to the couch. Alarmed at the paleness of her skin, he kept an arm circled around her waist until she settled on the sofa.

Patrick sat next to her, slid his arm behind her back and capping her shoulder blade with his hand, drew her close to his side. "Start at the beginning. Tell me everything."

Charlie leaned on him. Her hands trembled as she wiped tears off cheeks blotchy from crying. Breathing deeply, she stated in a monotone like she read from a grocery list, "I ignored my phone all morning. Then I saw the news. I figured Jamie was calling me about it. I listened to my voice mail. Emily left a message. She sounded excited, said she had fantastic news and wanted me to call her as soon as I got her message. I returned her call first. I was confused when a man answered her phone. I couldn't understand how my phone called the wrong number. I knew the voice but I couldn't place it."

Her voice a singsong, he worried about shock.

"Then he said he has..." A strangled sound and Charlie bent her head rocking back and forth. "He said he has my sister, but he doesn't want her. He wants me. He gave me three hours to find her and take her place."

She stopped talking and stared at him, her lavender eyes widening, swimming tears.

"Why does he want you specifically? The trial went his way."

"I don't know." She groaned and swiped the heel of her hand under her nose.

Accepting the handkerchief he drew out of his pants pocket, she dabbed under her eyes and then under her nose. "He hit on me after the trial. Obviously I turned him down."

"Okay. He can't handle the word *no*. What else did he say?"

"He told me to come alone. No cops, no help. Or Emily dies."

Her voice shook but she continued, "I agreed to

all that. I begged him to tell me *where*. How can I do as you say if you don't tell me where?"

Charlie shivered. "He said he doesn't care if I find him in time. Either way, I'm destroyed. He laughed then hung up the phone. I called her phone back, but it immediately went to voice mail. Then I called you. I don't know where to start. I don't know what to do. Please help me find her..." Her voice trailed off as she dissolved in tears. Sobs wracked her body, a series of tremors on the sofa.

"We'll find her." He held her face in his hands and used his thumbs to swab tears off her cheeks. "On my way over here Brian's fiancée, Matty, called me. She has, for lack of a better word, visions. She said she saw 'you' on the floor in a room with your hands bound."

"She knows where Emi is?" The glittering hope in her eyes tore his heart to shreds just as much as her tears had.

"No. But she also saw a totem pole. Large, full-scale with intricate carvings. Does this mean anything to you?"

"No." Charlie wagged her head, her eyes haunted, despairing.

"A sign on the pole read Lily's dream and the number two."

Her brows furrowed as she recited, "Lily's dream two." Charlie gasped. "Oh my God! The senator has a yacht named Lily's Dream. He named it after his late wife. I attended a campaign fund dinner on it a few months ago. That has to be it. He *has* to know where this is."

Patrick already had his phone out of his pocket. "And he sure as hell will tell me right now. Patch me through to Senator Morgan's office," Patrick commanded the police operator.

"Senator Morgan's office. How may I help you?" A woman responded.

"This is Captain Patrick Sullivan, CPD. I need to speak to the senator immediately."

"I am sorry, but that is not possible."

"This is an emergency. Official police business. This is not a request," Patrick stipulated. "I need the senator to come to the phone now."

"The senator's son died today. I cannot disturb him. Have a little respect." A dial tone sounded.

"Damn it, she hung up on me!" Incensed, Patrick hammered on a phone button to contact the operator again.

Charlie touched his sleeve lightly, her cell phone to her ear. "Hold on, Pat. I have an idea."

"What?"

She held her finger to her lips.

Charlie pressed a button and propped the phone against a large bowl in the center of the coffee table.

"Schotz, Pearson and Freemont. How may I direct your call?" came the greeting through the speaker.

"Hi Deb. It's C. J. I need to speak with Jamie. It's an emergency."

Patrick absently rubbed Charlie's back, her ribs prominent ridges through her flannel shirt. Little spasms skittered through the flesh beneath his fingers.

"Hold on C. J. I'll get him."

"Are you okay? Deb said it's an emergency." Jamie's voice was breathy as if he had sprinted to the phone.

"It is, Jamie. I need your help. In relation to Senator Morgan, does the phrase 'Lily's Dream Two' mean anything to you?"

"Yes. It's the name of his fishing cabin. My father took me to it once years ago. I don't remember much about it. I was just a kid."

"Do you remember where it was?"

"Wisconsin, I think. We must have that info in

his files somewhere. All the cabins had names. He named his after his first wife, just like his yacht. Father told me that it was bullshit. He hated his first wife. Strange thing, I do remember, though. There was a totem pole..."

Charlie's eyes widened as Patrick leaned forward closer to the speaker. "This is Captain Pat Sullivan, Jamie. It's imperative we have that address as soon as possible."

"Yeah, sure, Captain." Jamie's amiable tone vanished. "What's this about?"

"The senator's son kidnapped Emily and I think he took her to the cabin." Charlie's breath hitched and she squeezed her eyes shut.

Patrick circled an arm around her shoulder.

"What the hell! Emily's been kidnapped?" he bellowed. "Hold on..."

A clicking sound. "Deb, drop everything and pull Senator Morgan's file. I need it immediately. Thanks."

After another clicking sound, Jamie said, "It can't be Morgan, C. J. He's dead."

"That's what he wants everyone to believe. I wouldn't be surprised if he set that fire himself. That bastard is very much alive and he has my sister. I'm running out of time. I need to find him." Charlie rose from the sofa.

"Of course," Jamie agreed. "As soon as Deb brings the file..."

"Call my cell phone as soon as you have the address. We'll leave and drive the interstate north towards Wisconsin." Charlie swiveled her head towards him, eyebrows raised in question.

He nodded as he stood up next to her. "Let's go."

Scooping up her phone from the table, she stuffed it in her purse. A hand on her elbow, Patrick led her to the door and opened it. She tore through it and down the short hall to the elevator bank.

****

Patrick yanked the passenger handle on his car, swung it open and left it gaping for Charlie. Sprinting around the car, he heaved into the driver's seat, slammed his door closed and turned the ignition.

"No!" His rumbling engine and her shriek echoed hollow in the concrete parking garage.

"Charlie, get in the car," he demanded, a booming baritone that reverberated overloud.

"We *have* to take my car! He said *come alone!*" Charlie yelled. "Pat, *please...*"

Near hysteria garbled her last statement. The open passenger door framed the lower half of her body, swaying like a tree in a hurricane. He wasted no time arguing, grabbed a bubble light and the P25 portable radio and pitched back out of the car. Shoving her open door closed, he swung an arm around her waist and towed her to her parked 'Vette.

Easing her securely into the passenger seat, he rounded the car, plopped the beacon on its roof, switched it on and took the wheel. The engine roared and the siren blared, an earsplitting din in the enclosed garage. He reversed it out of the space and into drive with body-jerking rapidity. Speeding down the exit ramps in dizzying loops, tires whining, he broke into the straightaway toward the street entrance.

A cell phone chirped and she dug in her purse frantically. "Hello?

"Waterston, Wisconsin, off rural route 70," she recited. "Thanks, Jamie. Please say a prayer." Charlie hung up the phone and tossed it in her purse.

Preparing to cross the sidewalk fronting the garage driveway apron into the street, Patrick laid on the horn to warn pedestrians—as if the deafening siren weren't enough. His eyes tracked back and forth in rapid succession assuring clear passage and he rocketed into the street fishtailing into the lane.

Blowing through lights doing eighty plus on local streets, urgent necessity stole any sweetness in driving the collector's car of his dreams. Charlie's soft whimpers permeated his consciousness, but he couldn't console her until he mounted this critical operation.

Radioing dispatch, he barked, "Captain Sullivan in high speed approach on Ohio toward the Kennedy extension northbound. Driving civilian's car, 1966 Red Corvette, plates..." Patrick glanced at Charlie.

She fired out loud and clear, "BSB 3966."

"En route to 294 Junction to armed hostage situation near Waterston, Wisconsin. Patch me in to the commanding officer in the Waterston jurisdiction."

"Copy, Captain. Hold..." a female voice said.

Patrick dropped the portable in his lap, working the gearshift. Ascending the highway onramp along the shoulder, the tires chomping pebbles and blowing dust, he merged into the right lane, still in overdrive. The siren prompted drivers to swerve onto the right shoulder, letting him pass. Bumping around in her seat, Charlie covered her eyes with a hand.

Static crackled and the female dispatcher's voice squawked, "Sheriff Glen Summers connected, Captain Sullivan."

Patrick maneuvered into the far left lane and hit the gas. Eyes riveted to the road, accepting the right of way granted as the lane successively cleared ahead of him, he fished the radio out of his lap. "Sheriff, ETA in Waterston about eighty minutes. Can you supply SWAT backup and complete stealth for an abduction/ransom situation in a cabin in your jurisdiction? Live hostage in exchange for ransom.

Abductor is a suspected serial murderer, assumed armed and dangerous. I need your best sharpshooters. I'll take command..."

"Hold on, Captain. I *can* supply manpower. But it's not going to take me eighty minutes. Supply me details and we'll handle this," Summers asserted.

"The ransom is the hostage's identical sister," Patrick related.

Charlie mewled in agony; her sobbing shook the car console.

"She's with me in the car. The abductor stipulated that she goes in alone. The perp is the suspected Garbage Man Murderer. Hear about him in your neck of the woods?"

"No!" Charlie screamed. "What have I done? God, no!"

Miserable that he had added to her torment, Patrick continued. "We'll have minutes to finesse this and I'll need your best men under *my* command, Sheriff." His voice rang with authority.

"Yessir, Captain," the sheriff responded with the slightest trace of sarcastic inflection. "What's the location?"

"The cabin's named Lily's Dream Two. It's..."

"I know where Lily's Dream Two is," Summers interrupted, "in my neck of the woods."

Now the sarcasm had free rein.

"Assemble your men near the location and wait for me. Tell me where to meet you to plan the hostage exchange. This is time sensitive. We have until approximately four p.m. to send her sister in."

"There's a clearing in the woods in the cabin's vicinity. I'll have a cruiser waiting at the bottom of the off ramp to lead you there. Take the Four Lakes exit."

"I appreciate that. Over," Patrick signed off. Returning the portable radio to his lap, he clasped Charlie's hand while exerting steady pressure on the accelerator to maintain a speed of 120 mph.

Nothing more I can do until we get there.
Normally he'd clear his head prepping for action and
focus on executing the strategy. He worked blind
now. He had no knowledge of the terrain or whether
he could count on Summers' men and entrust them
with the precious life of the terrified, grief-bent
woman beside him. Or the life of the captive woman
who looked just like her.

"Charlie, sweetheart..." Patrick dangled his
right hand over the console and connected with her
left hand. So cold, a tiny ice cube. "We've got time.
We'll get there."

"I brought this on her. This is *my* fault. It's
always my fault," she exclaimed, her voice thick from
crying.

"Shhh..." Caressing her hand, he stroked it
gently. "I want to hold you in my arms, but I'd have
to stop the car. We can't afford it just now."

Continuing to massage her hand, he willed some
of his warmth into her quaking body, eyes trained on
the road. The 'Vette ate the highway, the white lane
strip a blur in the corner of his right eye.

"Do you want some soft music on the radio?" he
asked.

"No, no, no," she keened. "I can't bear music
right now—it's too much like her. Dear God!"

Her shoulders heaved as his useless hand
kneaded hers. "I'm going to fly apart," she whined.

"We can't afford that now, either," he advised,
his voice gentle, purposefully avoiding an accusing
tone. "Emily needs you to be calm to outwit this
scum."

"I know, I know..." Charlie heaved a sigh. "She's
needed me her whole life. The big sister." She
snorted.

"Your mom delivered you first?" he asked to
keep her talking, distract her.

168

Her nod registered in the corner of his eye. "I was always the leader, the brave one. I'd tell her what to do, even if it was naughty, and she'd fall in with the game plan, delighted. Always so happy to be with me. Always so trusting." She sniffled.

Pinching her cheeks, she swabbed a thumb and index finger under the wells of her eyes, wiping tears away. "I'm the books smart one. Emi hated school. She's always been a free spirit. As a kid, she'd sing and dance and spin circles in the yard while I'd sit in the grass with her script in my lap, trying to hold her still long enough to practice her lines for a school play. I'd demand like some kind of commanding officer, 'Em, *concentrate.*'"

Patrick grinned imagining the little girl foreshadowing the commanding litigator.

"She'd stop for five seconds while I ran a line," Charlie related. "And then she'd spin off again chanting hers while I'd dutifully search the script for the next line to feed her. Keep her on task. Instead of watching her dance. I should have watched her dance..." Her sobs wracked her body and rattled his arm, shaking him to the core.

Rocketing up the interstate his mind reeled. His Charlie was a panic-stricken sister who needed to muster every ounce of what made her unbeatable in the courtroom and take it to the door of that cabin in an hour. *How do I orchestrate this? I can't hide in the 'Vette. Wonder if Summers has thermal detection equipment? I have to keep Charlie out of the cabin— try to draw Morgan out. Separate him from Emily. Fuck, I wish I knew what surrounds the target.*

Serving in ATF, Patrick had extensive experience with hostage situations. Sheer guts had placed him directly in a shooter's crosshairs, hands up, headed into the target's holdout. With an ace SWAT team backing him up and a small concealed gun in a calf holster, he had neutralized the perpetrators two seconds after sweet-talking himself in the door. More than once. No matter how many scenarios he ran for neutralizing Morgan, he couldn't substitute Patrick Sullivan for Charlie Demarco in how he'd take the sick bastard down.

"I'm going to steal one of your lines here. Charlie, *concentrate*," Patrick suggested.

She sputtered a laugh, thankfully.

"When we size up the approach to the cabin, I'm going to give you *specific* instructions, understand?" He shook his head with an exasperated puff of air through his nostrils. "Problem is, I don't know what they are right now. But you have to follow them to *the letter*. It's the only way I'll let you go in there. Emily is counting on you."

A cruiser blasted into Patrick's lane a hundred yards ahead, sirens wailing. Assured of clear passage now, he flicked his eyes off the road for a second and faced her, needing eye-to-eye agreement.

Her irises were lavender pools fringed with red streaks. Mascara tracked muddy ribbons down her cheeks. Doe-eyed she nodded, her full lips quivering. "She has always counted on me and I always let her down."

Brows knit, he focused on the road and then glanced back at her. "You can do this, Charlie."

"I will." Her head bobbed.

Patrick concentrated on driving.

"I promise I won't be responsible for hurting her any more than I already have," Charlie said.

A loud sniff. "Before we moved to Chicago, we lived in northern New Jersey," she continued. "You could see the New York City skyline from Park Avenue in our town. Emi was Broadway bound. She even had a couple runs in off-Broadway productions under her belt. I had my own law firm with six associates. I handled everything—corporate law, estate planning, real estate and even divorce. I pretty much handled all litigation cases. I could pick and choose those cases I thought had merit. I loved every minute of the work. Since I wasn't in it to be rich, I did a ridiculous amount of pro bono work by most firms' standards."

"A penthouse overlooking Wrigley Field and this mighty fine car says rich to me, Counselor," he interjected.

"Huh. I'm getting to that."

Patrick glanced sideways, noticed her hands gripped in a white-knuckled ball in her lap.

"My firm hosted a huge charity fundraiser in the Trump Towers ballroom. Amazing press and attendance by the ultra wealthy in the metropolitan area, some celebrities and international money moguls. I met a man, *supposedly* one of those moguls, who... I dated him for several months and then accepted his proposal and a five-carat diamond ring. He was an investment wizard who made über-bucks for his clients. So it seemed. I entrusted him with virtually all my money, Emi's savings, and my parents' entire remaining life savings after they had spent hundreds of thousands on my college education. Even helped him attract other clients who invested with him because of my hearty endorsement. His name is Giovanni Renno. Ever hear of him?" she asked in a whisper.

Uck. Who hasn't? "Ponzi scheme. I think it's in Interpol's hands now."

"Correct. My firm went under because of client backlash. I lost credibility. My parents work in a grocery store now. And, you know that Emi lives with me. Jamie Freemont knew all this before he hired me, but my record as a litigator was flawless and high profile. He knew I needed the money desperately and he knew I'd deliver in the courtroom. He never once asked me to explain a thing about Giovanni. I owe him a great deal. I have worked like a slave so I could restore every penny of my family's money before Giovanni came into my life. But, because I chained myself to the job, I couldn't refuse the senator. And now..." She took a ragged breath. "My Emi..."

Charlie bent her head and cupped her face in her hands.

"I'm very attuned to her generous heart." Matty's pronouncement echoed in his mind. *"More to her than meets the eye..."*

The swell of passion Patrick experienced was ill timed. He couldn't take her in his arms, stroke her silky mane of hair and cover her with kisses to stamp her with his love, given freely. Something she could trust, rely on...forever.

"Charlie, I *do* love you," he professed with a squeeze of his hand.

Charlie sniffed and her breath caught with a mewling sound. Then she replied, "I *do* love you, too, Pat."

The swell of elation staggered him. No woman had ever pronounced her love to him. Even if that weren't true, only this woman counted.

"We'll be there soon. You have to let me take over then. Can you do that?"

"Yes," she promised.

"All right." Patrick gave a quick nod.

"I don't care about myself. Tell me Emi will be all right," Charlie whimpered.

With a hard squeeze on her hand, he proclaimed, "Emily *will be* all right. *And so will you.*"

Silent, they careened down the highway, as he held her hand cradled in her lap.

Tailing the cruiser, Patrick veered over two lanes and down the exit ramp, a near lift-off. The cruiser switched off the siren using only the lights to warn drivers of their speedy approach on more local roads, and Patrick followed suit.

As they turned onto a dirt path thickly forested on either side, Charlie remarked, "By the way, Giovanni's diamond was a zircon."

Chapter 19

Relief coursed through Patrick's veins as he surveyed the manpower in the clearing from his seat in the 'Vette. Sheriff Summers, true to his word, stood next to a black-and-white squad car, feet planted, beefy arms crossed over an ample belly. Nondescript sedans squeezed in the limited space in the clearing next to the dirt drive that Patrick presumed led to the cabin.

Charlie's eyes widened as she fixated on the paramedic rig parked diagonally across a patch of grass, rear tires in the main access road.

Patrick squeezed her hand for reassurance. "It's just a precaution, Charlie."

She managed a wan smile and straightened her shoulders. Her C. J. Demarco persona in place, she opened the passenger door. A damp breeze wafted into the car. She climbed out and trod a few feet to the edge of the dirt road as if approaching the jury box. Charlie stood erect, unmoving, staring down the road. *She's ready to wage the battle of her life.*

Turning, she drifted toward him as he exited the car, a blank, haunted cast in her red-streaked eyes. Patrick's pulse escalated observing her, hyper-aware of the stakes in this operation. Birds chirped and squirrels jumped from branch to branch overhead, oblivious to the drama unfolding beneath them.

Patrick paced toward the sheriff carrying the portable radio in one hand, the other outstretched in greeting. "Pat Sullivan."

"Glen Summers, Sullivan." He pumped Patrick's hand twice.

"This is Charlie Demarco, the hostage's twin," Patrick remarked as Charlie delivered a firm handshake to the sheriff.

"Ma'am." Summers unrolled a map and spread it flat on the hood of his squad car. Doors opened as the SWAT team emerged from the sedans. Leaving the car doors ajar, the men formed a huddle around Patrick and the sheriff and scrutinized the aerial map.

"We are here." A pudgy finger pointed to the clearing on the map. "The cabin is about a quarter of a mile down that road. There are two outbuildings over here and here."

Patrick concentrated on the map as Charlie leaned against his side.

"There is no tree coverage by the outbuildings." Patrick shook his head. "Our best bet is to position guns here and here." He tapped the map with an index finger. "I'll take up position behind this cluster of trees. Check radio frequency," Patrick concluded holding out the P25.

The team fiddled with portable radios.

"He said to come alone." Charlie glared at him.

"He won't detect us. I promise you." Patrick rubbed a hand on her back.

One by one, the SWAT team moved toward command posts, disappearing like specters into the forest around the clearing.

Leading Charlie toward her car, Patrick conveyed urgent instructions. "Wait five minutes so we can position and then I want you to slowly drive towards the cabin. No more than ten miles per hour. Stop in front of the cabin and turn off the engine. Honk the horn. Do not get out of the car. Make him come to you. Don't unlock the doors. We have to try to lure him out."

"Okay." She slid into the driver's seat.

Patrick leaned inside the car, one arm over the

doorframe. "I mean it, Charlie," he reiterated. If he doesn't come out, we'll go in. We don't want to give him two hostages. Understand?"

Nodding, she grasped the handle and he moved away to allow her to shut the door. Both hands on the wheel, she stared straight ahead. He wanted to fling the door open, pull her into his arms and never let go.

Patrick left the clearing, reluctant but on task. Emotions had never clouded duty before and he couldn't permit it, especially now. But every instinct opposed using the woman he loved as bait. Turning, he slipped between the trees. There wasn't time to mount this operation another way. He would not look back or he'd drag her out of the car.

Patrick's eyes rapidly adjusted to the dim light. The other men circled the cabin—only a blur of occasional movement in his peripheral vision— shadows that seemed to blend with the scenery. Adrenaline pumped through his blood. Sweat trickled down his hairline. Blocking out the sounds of soft rustling in the underbrush, the occasional acorn plops on the forest floor, he focused acutely on freeing Emily and capturing Morgan. And protecting Charlie at all costs.

In position behind a towering evergreen tree, the scent of pine tickled his nose. He knelt in a bed of pine needles, his eyes trained on the log cabin in front of him. *Matty's winning streak is intact.* The towering totem pole was situated next to the tilting porch. The front door stood open. No movement. No lights within. The cabin appeared deserted, but Patrick sensed Morgan's demented presence prickling the skin on the back of his neck.

Summers crouched next to him. For a big man he moved like smoke. He held a blueprint in his hand. Silently he handed it over. The diagram showed the cabin's simple floor plan: the first floor primarily open space with a small bedroom in the back of the house, framed out next to the living room.

Patrick tensed as Charlie's tires crunched over stones in the dirt road. She stopped the car about twenty feet from the porch and switched off the engine. Facing toward the cabin, she sat unmoving behind the wheel. *Good girl. Don't get out of the car. Now lay on the horn.*

Charlie opened the car door, swung her legs out and stood at the side of the 'Vette. *Damn it. No! Stay in the car!*

No movement from the cabin.

A blood-curdling scream drowned out the chirping birds. The hair stood up on Patrick's forearms. Charlie broke into a run toward the open door. *No. No. No! Damn it. Don't go in there! That's what he wants.* Patrick sprang into the open on a bead for her, determined to tackle her if necessary. He came up short.

Disappearing through the front door, she screamed, "Don't hurt her! I'm here!"

Bounding up the porch steps in one stride, his lips against the radio mouthpiece, Patrick commanded, "Close flanks around the perimeter. I'm going in."

Tossing the radio off the porch, he drew his gun. *I'll be lucky if I have a clear shot.* One chance.

He cleared the front door in a low crouch and followed the sound of sobbing to the back of the house. Pressed against the wall, his pistol clutched with both hands against his chest, finger on the trigger, he peered into the bedroom with one eye. Charlie presented her back to him about two feet into the room. Morgan was situated near the back wall of the room, far left, shielded from the window on the right wall by the open closet door.

He held Emily off the ground, her face directly

in front of his, by one muscled arm around her waist, a knife at her throat. Her thin arms bound in front of her with duct tape, she wriggled and then went limp intermittently. Tears streamed down her face as she whimpered, breathing in hitches. A piece of loose duct tape dangled from the side of her puffy lips, one eye swollen shut.

"You bitch," Morgan addressed Charlie, his face still hidden behind Emily. "You think you can laugh at me and get away with it? You think you are so much better than me, don't you?" He jutted his head to the side, his face distorted with rage.

Patrick's arm muscles twitched, poised to take the shot, but Morgan moved his head again and Emily flailed in his grasp. *Hold still. Hold still. Come on you bastard—show your face.*

"Just let her go," Charlie begged. "You don't want her. I'm the one who laughed at you. She didn't. You can have me. I will do anything you want. Just let her go." Charlie edged forward a couple inches further blocking his shot.

"Don't get any closer." A thin line of blood appeared on Emily's neck as Morgan indented soft skin with the point of the blade. "Do you think it's going to be that easy? The high and mighty C. J. Demarco will just waltz in and get her own way as usual? Fuck you. This is my courtroom and I am the judge. You lose."

He hoisted Emily higher off the ground, his bicep bulging as he squeezed her chest.

"Charlie, run," Emily wailed. "He's going to kill us both."

Through the window, Patrick's eyes connected with one of Summers' men. Patrick blinked three times conveying they would go on three. One, two— on the third blink the glass shattered.

Lord be with me.

Emily jerked her head away from the window,

baring Morgan's face as Patrick stepped into the doorway and squeezed the trigger. The earsplitting shot exploded Morgan's head, spraying the wall behind him with bloody pulp.

The women screamed.

Emily crumpled to the floor, Morgan's body at angles with hers. Hysterically crying, Charlie flung forward onto her knees, shoved the corpse off Emily's legs and cradled her in her lap, rocking.

SWAT swarmed through the front door, guns drawn.

Patrick holstered his gun and knelt, wrapping his arms around the sisters. "It's over. You're okay now. He's gone," he said. "It's over."

Heartbeat steadying, Patrick held them, grateful for the trembling warmth of their bodies, the faint aroma of gardenias from his Charlie's perfume.

Musty odors and the metallic pungent scent of Morgan's blood and gunpowder added to the mix.

Summers ambled in front of him, glanced at the corpse and then up over Patrick's head. "Get the EMTs in here for her," he demanded.

"I've got her," Patrick replied. Rising, he towed Charlie up with him, made sure she was steady on her feet. He bent at the knees and picked Emily up in his arms. Charlie grabbed Emily's hand and Patrick moved forward, shielding their view of the lifeless body.

Outside, red flashing lights swirled through the trees as the paramedics drove the rig down the driveway. Patrick held Emily tightly against his chest until the stretcher rolled in front of him and then carefully placed her on the crisp white sheets. The paramedics surrounded her.

Charlie leaned her head against Patrick's chest, panting lightly. "Thank you sounds so insignificant," she said in a breathy voice. "I don't think I could live if anything happened to Emily because of me." Her shudder reverberated through him. "You will never know how thankful I am."

I couldn't live if I let anything happen to you. "I know..." Tipping his finger under her chin, he tilted her head up to meet his lips. Lost, a rush of heightened sensation quickened his pulse, similar to the adrenaline surge minutes before—but infinitely better. He lingered in the kiss. For the moment, the cabin, the paramedics, the horror that it could have gone another way receded.

Ending the kiss, he whispered, "I love you. I would do anything for you." He wrapped her in his arms. Her head nestled against his chest. Eyes closed, he rested his chin on top of her head, her soft hair brushing his neck. "I had to keep you safe."

Not that you listened worth a damn. His hands on her shoulders, he said, "I told you not to get out of the car, didn't I?"

Her head jerked up, that bratty glint of ready warfare in her mesmerizing lavender eyes. Patrick smiled, thankful for the high color in her cheeks. "Don't argue with me," he admonished her. "You won't win this one."

She huffed a sigh. "When Emi screamed, I had to run to her. I was terrified. I couldn't stop."

"I forgive you this time."

"Forgive me?" Charlie's voice rose.

One of the men interrupted, "Sir." *Probably lucky she didn't get the chance to deliver that closing argument.* "I think you should see what we found inside."

The paramedics loaded the stretcher in the truck. Charlie bit her bottom lip and rushed over to the nearest man, "Where are you taking her?"

"St. Joe's, ma'am. No reason for concern. She has deep bruises and will need stitches on her eye. We'll need an X-ray of her wrist. It may be fractured."

"Can I ride with her?" Charlie inquired, her voice strained.

"Sure."

She turned to face him. Patrick smiled and promised, "I'll call you later."

"Please do," she responded with a wide smile, her eyes twinkling.

Patrick joined her by the rig, reached for Charlie's hand and clasped it.

Kissing the knuckles and then wrapping ten fingers around his hand, she declared, her voice thick with emotion, "Thank you for everything."

Charlie climbed in the back of the rig next to the stretcher. Patrick reluctantly closed the doors. He stood in the middle of the drive as the truck moved away, stationary until he could no longer see its brake lights.

Patrick turned toward Summers' man waiting at the bottom of the porch steps. "Show me what you found."

"Follow me, sir. It's upstairs."

Patrick stomped through the front door and up the stairs behind him. Then he stood in the hallway peering into the indicated room: a macabre trophy room judging from the "wallpaper." Newspaper articles covered an entire wall. Crossing the threshold, Patrick headed toward the wall and scanned the newsprint: headlines of the Garbage Man slayings scotch taped in a frayed, grisly découpage. A collection of wood baseball bats were stacked on the closet floor like wine bottles in a cooler.

He walked over to a chipped wooden dresser topped with two framed pictures: a newspaper picture of C. J. Demarco straight-faced at the side of Jackson Morgan III and a black-and-white photo of a woman holding a delicate, curly-headed child's hand—hard to determine if it was male or female.

"In here, Captain," a male voice called.

Patrick followed it and encountered Summers in the hallway pointing toward an open door. Striding toward him, Patrick entered the small bathroom. The door on the medicine cabinet hung open, its three shelves lined with prescription bottles. Picking one up, he read the label. Checking each bottle consecutively yielded the same information about the vials' contents. *Testosterone.*

Chapter 20

Early October

The trolley lurched to a halt and the members of the wedding party hopped off single file. Scattered showers that morning had miraculously stopped minutes before to grant the bride and groom this photo opportunity.

Charlie knelt down, flanked by Bobbie and Molly, to gather up handfuls of the champagne satin bridal train so Matty could travel the path strewn with damp leaves toward her wish list wedding picture spot. Once Matty's dainty ivory sandals planted on stone, the bridesmaids lowered the train and the bride swept up to meet Brian on the crest of the arched bridge.

Emily joined Charlie and leaned on the stone railing at the base of the bridge. "Have you ever seen such a starry-eyed pair?" Emily gazed at Matty and Brian with an amused expression.

Charlie observed the couple posing for the photographer. Blazing fall colors painted the tree line behind them and sunshine broke through the clouds casting dappled light on the bride and groom. "It was a gorgeous wedding. They're truly meant for each other."

"Speaking of gorgeous." Emily turned away from the railing and nodded her head to the right.

Charlie twisted her neck, peering over her shoulder to where the Sullivan brothers congregated.

"Will you just *look* at those men. One is hotter

than the next." Emily fanned her face and glanced at Charlie, a keen glint in her eyes. "Especially your big hunky cop." she smirked.

"I *do* love that man," Charlie declared, her eyes lingering on Pat. Clad in a black tuxedo and an ivory shirt with a copper-colored rose boutonnière he looked impossibly handsome. *I can't wait until we're alone tonight.*

Charlie's eyes roamed and noticed Jamie Freemont chatting with John Sullivan. "How about your man, sis? Jamie looks fantastic today, too."

Emily grinned. "I *do* like that man." She leaned on the railing again elbow to elbow with Charlie. "I'll see what happens with him once I'm back in New York. He says he'll be at every Saturday performance. I'd like that."

Charlie wagged her head, a hollow sensation in her chest. "I'm going to miss you so much. But I'm so *very* proud of you. You are fantastic in the part. I almost explode with pride every time I see you on stage. *Parkview Life* will be a smash hit on Broadway, I just know it."

Emily huffed a laugh. "From your mouth to God's ears. Then maybe I can take care of you and Mom and Dad instead of your shouldering the expenses."

Charlie frowned.

"Don't look at me that way." Emily bumped Charlie's elbow playfully. "You're poverty stricken as a prosecutor compared to the salary Jamie paid you."

Nodding, Charlie grinned. "And I've never been happier in my life." She glanced over her shoulder indicating Jamie. "Except when I have to face him in a courtroom."

Emily laughed heartily, pointing an index finger. "Will you look at those two?"

The Lynch twins minced on tiptoe as if they navigated a bed of hot coals instead of damp leaves, little hands hitching up their Laura Ashley flower girl dresses. "Don't they remind you of us?"

The kids blended with a group of relatives next to Kay Lynch who chatted with the Sullivan and Demarco parents, doting grandparents both legit and honorary. Since the ordeal in the hospital while Emi had recuperated from what turned out to be internal injuries, Charlie's parents had instantly been folded into the clan.

Charlie gazed at the swirling water below, the waterfalls a rushing cascade in the near distance. She shivered contemplating the reason why Matty and Brian had insisted on shooting their wedding pictures here. Matty had related the treacherous incident on the bridge that almost cost her life until Brian saved the day. An icy chill ran through Charlie at the memory of the terrifying events at the cabin a couple months ago. Until Pat saved her…and her precious sister.

Guilt still plagued Charlie over her unwitting defense of the Garbage Man Murderer. But she derived consolation and a large measure of pleasure anticipating the day when she'd prosecute ex-Senator Morgan in the upcoming months— obstruction of justice in the Shirlee Davis case, the least of possible charges. Pat's investigation had uncovered a possible homicide a little over twenty years ago that he believed linked to the Morgans—a missing prostitute whose services may have been a sixteenth birthday present from father to son. Lily Snelling, the first Mrs. Morgan, currently in a psychiatric institution, had alluded to it during questioning. She had also divulged the senator's unyielding insistence that their hermaphrodite baby had to be raised male.

Leaves scuffled as the Sullivans mounted the bridge for family photos. Pat drew near and crooked his elbow, a gentleman's stance. "Time to smile for the camera."

Charlie beamed at him, linking her arm through his. Just touching him grounded her, yet spun her off center with longing. Usually a citizen of the attorney's world of logic, her illogical emotions for Pat didn't bother her one bit.

"Have I told you you look stunning today?" he asked, cocking an eyebrow, his dimples blooming with a wide smile.

"I seem to recall...but you can tell me again." She chuckled and ran a hand down the skirt of her copper-hued satin gown. "I'm still honored Matty asked me to be a bridesmaid."

"Member of the fam now," he said casually.

They strolled up the stone arch and assembled as directed by the photographer. Pat behind her, his warm hands rested gently on her waist, his breath on the back of her neck sending tingles of pleasure through her.

"Okay, everybody," the photographer aimed the camera, one hand in the air. "On three."

It's easy to smile for the camera here with him. Everything's easy with him.

The bridesmaids swooped near Matty for the reverse trip back to the trolley. Pat trailed Charlie as she held her portion of the bridal train off the ground. "Now for the party," he said.

"Just don't make me sing," Charlie insisted.

"I think your talented sister has that covered." Pat winked at Emily.

****

Charlie's experience attending weddings included opposite extremes. If the party was so-so, the event dragged on endlessly. The good parties ended seemingly minutes after they had started. From her seat at the longest head table she'd ever seen, Charlie wished she could rewind the evening that would end soon. It did seem as if they had just arrived at the arboretum for the reception.

A row of tea lights flickered in front of her and down the length of the table. Sweet scents of roses and freesia floated from the bridal bouquets set in ornate tussie mussies on pedestal stands at the bridesmaids' places at the table. Pat crossed the dance floor toward her and the candlelight reflected stars in his dreamy blue eyes. She rose as he reached the table, smiling with delight as he warmed the palm of her hand with a kiss.

"Would you like to dance, Charlie? Or how about a walk outside?"

She glanced over her shoulder out the wall of windows that the head table fronted. A full harvest moon cast pale yellow light on the waters of a pond rimmed with evergreens, fiery red-leafed maples and lemon-colored ginkgo trees. "I'd love to walk around the grounds."

Outside, Pat slipped off his jacket and wrapped it around her shoulders. Recalling the same gesture on the end of Navy Pier had her smiling at the memory of their first date. Leaves crackled underfoot as they strolled, the brisk air fanning her face. "This is the most beautiful place," she remarked. "The church was magnificent. Honestly, I don't think I've ever been to a prettier wedding."

Grinning up at Pat, she confided, "Joe's toast was hilarious."

He snorted. "I'm going to ask Brian to be the best man when I get married. With Joe, it's more a roast than a toast."

"When *you* get married?" She narrowed her eyes.

"You know..." He winked. "One day."

Halting, Pat remarked, "I think we better get back. Matty's going to throw the bouquet."

"Uck," Charlie grimaced. "I'll pass on that."

"Uh—" He hesitated. "Okay, then it's Plan C."

"Huh?"

Swiveling his head, he seemed to search the vicinity and focused on a bench near the pond. "Want to sit for a while?"

"Sure." She trod over thick grass and settled on the bench next to him, his long muscular leg like a line of hard rock against the side of her thigh. Sighing contentedly, she held his huge hand in her lap. No longer reluctant for the wedding to end, she thought about what his hands would kindle in her body in the hotel room later.

Crossing her feet at the ankles, she relaxed on the bench, but Pat sat erect staring at her.

Shaking his head a couple times, he licked his lips and then said, "Maybe I should have gone with Plan A, but it just seemed too...I don't know...staged." He chuckled.

"But Plan B had possibilities. At least they all thought so," he continued.

"What in the world are you talking about?" She gazed at him, baffled.

"Okay." His eyes locked on hers, a determined expression on his handsome face. "I love you, Charlie."

Smiling, she furrowed her brows. "I love you, too."

"I want forever, Charlie. With you. Will you marry me?" He dug inside his pocket and withdrew a small, black velvet box.

Her heart froze as he opened the lid, moonlight glinting on the solitaire inside. "My God." She hung over the box, breathless, temporarily paralyzed.

Lifting the ring out, he clasped her hand tenderly, slid the delicate band just over the nail on her ring finger and paused, his eyes wide, searching hers.

Tears welled as she finally found her voice, "Yes! Oh, yes, Pat. I love you so much."

His fingers eased the ring securely in place and she fell into his arms, head pressed on his shoulder, her heart beating wildly. Raising her head, she met his lips and sealed the promise, tasting champagne on his tongue.

Excitement bubbling inside her, she held fast to his hand as they hurried back toward the building.

"Plan A was a proposal at the intermission of Emily's debut in the play when your parents were in town," Pat related. "Everybody thought it would be a sensational way to mark the day. But I didn't want to take away from Emi's moment, even though she insisted."

"Emily *knows* about this?" *Not even the tiniest hint this whole time!*

Pat grinned. "Plan B involved all the single ladies racing off the dance floor once Matty tossed the bouquet straight at you. Then I was supposed to drop to one knee."

Charlie burst out laughing. "I am *so* glad you went with Plan C."

Pat pecked her lips with a soft kiss as he held the door open for her. "Let's go tell them our news."

Arm in arm, they strolled into the reception hall. Charlie's amusement increased as she noticed the succession of eager glances and piqued attention from the family. Slowly she extended her left arm in front of her holding her engagement ring on display. The gesture caused a domino effect of grins, mumbling, and passed on remarks among the bunch of them.

Emily raced across the ballroom and launched into a balance-threatening hug with Charlie. "Oh, sweetie! I'm so happy for you!" she exclaimed. She planted a kiss on Charlie's cheek.

Pat swept her into an embrace. He kissed her passionately leaving her weak-kneed and elated when their lips parted.

His arm around her waist, Charlie met her mom's tear-filled eyes across the room as Pat's brothers herded together on the dance floor. On Joe's downbeat snap of the fingers they chanted, "Another one bites the dust."

About the Author

Sisters, Pat Casiello and Kathie Clare write as K. M. Daughters. Their penname is dedicated to the memory of their parents, Kay and Mickey, the "K" and "M" in K. M. Daughters. *All's Fair in Love and Law* is the fourth book in the author's acclaimed Sullivan Boys Romantic Suspense Series. K. M. Daughters writes romantic suspense for The Wild Rose Press and inspirational romance for White Rose Publishing.

Contact K. M. Daughters at
http://www.kmdaughters.com

Thank you for purchasing
this Wild Rose Press publication.
For other wonderful stories of romance,
please visit our on-line bookstore at
www.thewildrosepress.com

For questions or more information,
contact us at
info@thewildrosepress.com

The Wild Rose Press
www.TheWildRosePress.com

LaVergne, TN USA
07 November 2010
203876LV00001B/1/P